BAD, BUT *Perfectly* **GOOD** *At It*

ACKNOWLEDGEMENTS

I'm going to keep this short and sweet because Lord knows I could write a whole book on people I want to acknowledge. First and foremost I wanna give all the glory, honor, and praise to God! I want everyone to know that if you put God first in your life and have 100% faith and trust in Him YOU CAN DO ANYTHING!! I would be nothing without my Heavenly Father and his son Jesus. If you didn't know now you know! To the lovely Ms. Jessica Watkins, shout out to you for puttin' me on lol! Seriously though I can't thank you enough for giving me a shot at making my dreams come true. I appreciate all your words of advice and encouragement throughout this entire process. To the ladies at JWP y'all are amazing!! MAMA I MADE IT!! Lol ☺ I have to give props to my mommy and daddy for putting their lives and dreams on hold to make sure me and my brothers came up in the best way possible. It's because of y'all and the rest of the fam that I am the woman I am today. I love my grandmas and granddad so much for playing a part in raising us up. Thank y'all for having me in church every Sunday even if I didn't want to go. ☺ Shout out to my Blackwell family and Williams family. Jasiah and Jayla, my babies, there are no words meaningful enough to describe how much I love y'all. I would go to the ends of the earth and back for you two. Every day I look into your faces and tell myself I gotta be successful. Y'all are my motivation. To the love of my life D'Shawn, I couldn't imagine doing any of this without you. When everyone else doubted me and said I couldn't do it, you spoke life into me. You pray for me, continue to be patient with me, and teach me so much. When I'm down you're there, when I'm up you're there. Not only for me but for my kids too. I know that you have my back like no other and I love you for that. To my true definitions of real friends I love, love, love you ladies. My friends haven't left my side no matter what the situation was. They supported, uplifted, and motivated me to do what it is I'm supposed to be doing in my life. I love that we can keep it real with each other and still be the best of friends after it's all said and done. I love how y'all have been there for me throughout this entire process making sure that I never lost track of my vision. Kendraaaa man if it wasn't for you this book would still be on paper lol I owe you a brand new lap top baby!! Mesha thank you for keeping me in touch with the Holy Spirit when I be ready to go Colombo on people lmbo. The two people I have known for the shortest amount of time showed me that true friendship isn't about how long you known a person but who never left your side. My sister Elichawa (she gonna kill me lol) has been there since day 1 and no matter what we go through you have proved to me that you will always be there for me. You're like the big sister I never asked for but I thank God that I have you and wouldn't trade you for the world. Can't forget about my little sister Lyasia, one of the most loyal people I know and loyalty is everything. To all my Day 1's that I still remain close to after all this time I haven't forgotten about y'all. We may not talk or see each other every day but I see y'all and I thank y'all for the support. I will forever love my Pine Oaks crew. Special shout out to Ashley, Moncy, Tiara, and Courtney!!! If I have forgotten anyway it's not because I don't love you, it's because it's too many people to name but I love all of y'all!! I love and appreciate everyone that has supported me and I hope you guys enjoy my first book!!

JESSICA WATKINS PRESENTS
Bad, But Perfectly Good At It

JASMINE WILLIAMS

CHAPTER 1

Silina

It was 1:45 am when I arrived at the Norfolk International Airport. I was on my way home to surprise my husband, Chief, and show him how much I appreciated him. It was because of him that I was able to open my third clothing boutique. I had one in my hometown Virginia, New York, and now Miami. Chief was there for the grand opening of the store in Miami and he took me out on the town to celebrate that night. I couldn't celebrate as much as I would have liked to because I was carrying our child, but he still showed me a wonderful time. He left the next day saying that he had to get back to business, and I stayed in Miami for the next few days to make sure that my store was off to a good start. I couldn't wait to get into the arms of my man after the last week of all work and no play.

Chief was the love of my life. I had never met a better man. He showed me what it was like to love somebody with your whole heart and he genuinely loved me just as much. He was such a gentleman when I met him, and it has stayed that way. He didn't lock me down and then switch up on me like most dudes did. He always stayed consistent.

I loved the fact that he was a thug and a gentleman. I needed somebody that could protect me if something went down, and that was him all day long. I knew that he would kill somebody behind me if it came down to it. With me, he was romantic, charming, charismatic, and an overall good man. In the streets, niggas knew not to fuck with him. He could be a ruthless motherfucker when it came down to his money. He never did his dirty work around me or even discussed certain situations with me either. He thought that it was better that way, but of course the streets were always talking.

When we first met, there was an undeniable chemistry between us. As cliché as it may sound, I knew he was the one from the moment we laid eyes on each other. I was drawn in by his conversation. He was a very intelligent and wise man. He stimulated my mind more than anything, and I was learning a lot from him. We went on romantic dates at least twice a week, he took me on shopping sprees out of town, and we traveled the world. I saw things I had never seen and visited places I had never been.

It took a real man to step up and love another man's children, and he did. It was the thing I loved the most about him. He loved and treated my three daughters like they were his own—even better than their real father ever could. I loved that man more than life itself. He was more than my husband, he was my best friend. The fact that he was fine as hell put the icing on the cake. My husband was a full blood Indian which is how he got the nick name Chief. He was red with that soft, milky skin tone. He had deep waves in his hair and they were natural waves, not the kind that came from all those greasy ass products. He had broad shoulders, a wide chest, and an eight–pack. His body was built like one of those football players, and I loved it. Not to mention the man was rich. I didn't want or need him for his money, though. There's one thing about me. I always made sure I had my own. I just wanted love and loyalty, but I *was* glad that he could provide me with the lifestyle that I worked hard to live. It was nothing worse than lying up with a man that couldn't do anything for you, or bring more to the table than what you already have.

The walk from the airport exit to my car in the freezing cold weather was damn near unbearable. With every breath I took you could see the fog coming out of my mouth as if I was exhaling smoke from a cigarette. The wind caused my eyes to tear up, and the tears froze on my cheeks before they even got a chance to fall. The snow started to come down hard and it began to blanket the streets, sidewalks, and grass. When it snowed in Virginia it was a big hassle because the state never prepared the roads and the people here couldn't drive when it was bright and sunny outside, let alone in the snow. I shivered and wrapped my arms snuggly around myself in attempt to get some warmth. The cold was definitely not my cup of tea.

As I was walking up to my car, I hit the unlock button on my keychain, and a strange feeling came over me. My gut was telling me that something wasn't right. It was that nagging feeling that you get when you know that something is about to go down, but I couldn't put my finger on it. I decided to just brush it off. I pulled off from the airport in my cocaine white 2014 Infinity M45, aka my pretty bitch, Co–Co. It wasn't anything too fancy, but I didn't want to attract too much unwanted attention since my husband was a big time hustler. With the money I was making at my boutiques, I could easily afford the lifestyle that I was living. I just didn't want to give the cops any reason to be all up in my business. We all know they are quick to want to investigate a black person in a nice car. It was better to be safe than sorry in my eyes.

I pulled up in front of my five bedroom home in Chesapeake and got out of my car. The bitter, winter wind hit me hard and damn near pushed my 5'2" 120 pound ass to the ground. It was biting outside, and was so cold that the skin on my face began to tighten up. I could feel the goose bumps starting to pop up all over my body.

When I entered the house, I didn't even bother to cut on the lights. I also made sure to be as quiet as possible so I wouldn't wake anyone. I used the light from my cell phone to guide me to the kitchen so I could make myself a cup of tea before I went to bed. I drank at least one cup of chamomile tea a day, because it helped to ease my mind and made me relax. When I put the water on the stove and went to go sit down on one of my barstools, suddenly, the house was no longer silent. The quiet was replaced with a steady squeaking and headboard banging, followed by moaning. At least I *could have sworn* that was what I heard. But I had to make sure I wasn't hearing things, so I went up the stairs to investigate and to find out exactly what the hell was going on.

"I know one of these little heifers ain't bold enough to actually be fucking a nigga in a house that they live in with me," I whispered to myself as I ascended the stairs. I was prepared to curse one of my daughters out if what I thought was confirmed. Grown or not, no child of mine was going to be fucking in my house. That was something I took seriously.

The closer I got to the top of the stairs, the louder the headboard and moaning got. It confirmed that somebody was definitely getting it in in my house, and I was going to find out which one of them had the balls to do it.

"Oh shit, girl, fuck! I love the way you ride this dick," he exclaimed.

It sounded like one of my husband's expressions. *I know I'm not tripping. Oh fuck nah I know this nigga ain't*, I thought to myself.

Whatever was going on, I wanted to catch him in the act. I moved so damn fast up the steps that I lost my footing and slid down about three of them. Out of instinct I put my hand on my stomach and prayed I didn't cause any harm to my 12–week–old fetus. I experienced so many different emotions in a split second. Just the thought of my man fucking somebody else in our house–let alone in our bed–had me ready to go on a rampage. I hadn't witnessed anything with my own two eyes yet, but just hearing it was tearing me apart. To say I was hurt would be an understatement. The tears had already started welling up in my eyes before I even got to see what was going on. A part of me didn't even want to go in the room because I knew my heart wouldn't be able to take seeing him giving away the love and affection that was supposed to be designated only for me.

I was afraid of having to accept the reality that my man was no different than any of the other no good ass niggas. More than anything I was afraid of what the fuck I would do to him and whoever he had the nerve to bring up in my spot. The heart–tugging, devastating pain that I began to feel quickly turned to curiosity because I just had to find out who this nigga had the audacity to be fucking in my crib. *He obviously forgot what type of bitch he was fucking with*, I thought to myself.

I took a deep breath and braced myself before I peeped through the door that they didn't even have the decency to close. My heart sank into the pit of my stomach as I took a step back and grabbed my chest. What I saw before me damn near drove me to the brink of insanity. I felt my heart shatter into a million pieces. I busted through the door instantly, almost taking that bitch off the hinges.

The first thing I saw was my daughter Milan bouncing up and down on my man's dick like a pogo stick. When Chief looked up and saw me coming toward the two of them like a crazed lunatic, his eyes got as wide as two half dollars. Milan whipped her head toward the door, and with a stunned look on her face she instantly jumped off of Chief.

"Ba–baby," Chief stuttered.

Before Milan could even fix her mouth to speak, I punched her right square in her nose. She tried to fight back, but she didn't stand a chance against me. I roughly grabbed her hair and wrapped my wrist around it to keep her head still. While I was tugging on her hair and punching her, she fell off the foot of the bed. I felt like I had Hulk strength, the way I was mopping the floor with her ass. It was true when they say 'Sometimes you don't know your own strength'. I was tossing my daughter, who outweighed me by at least twenty pounds, around like she was a damn rag doll. Chief saw that Milan was about to kick me in my stomach. He grabbed her by her ankle and twisted her body into an awkward position.

"This some bullshit! You were *just* fucking me and telling me you love me, now you tryna protect her!" Milan screeched while getting up off the floor.

Chief was at a loss for words. All he could do was stand there and look sappy.

"Really, Chief, you love *her*? If you love that lil' thing over there then I know I'm too much woman for you. The only thing you love is pussy, money, and those drugs!" I shouted. I was trying to remain calm for my unborn baby, but I was becoming too overwhelmed.

"Well that's obviously a lie," Milan muttered.

"Shut the fuck up, Milan! You're making shit worse than it already is," Chief growled. "Look baby, let's sit down and talk without all the distractions."

By this time I heard enough of the bullshit. I was so pissed that I reached behind me and grabbed a razor blade from the dresser. I did it with such quickness that Chief never even saw it coming until the blade came down on his face. I sliced his red ass from his forehead to his chin, right along his right cheek. His face immediately split open, and blood instantly started pouring out of the open wound.

"Aaaahhh!" He shrieked.

His hand quickly jerked to the bloody gash on his face, and when he looked at it and saw all the blood, he charged at me like he was about to rip my ass to shreds. Before he could do anything to me, he stopped himself. He must have realized that if he put his hands on me right then he probably would have killed me and the baby he was just trying to protect. We both knew that he didn't want or need to catch that type of case. We just stared at each other for what seemed like forever, with menacing glares, watching and waiting to see who was going to make the next move. As I was watching him, I noticed that he seemed to be getting lightheaded from the pain mixed with losing all that blood.

"Ouch! That gotta hurt, Chief. Ain't it funny how the one you were trying to protect just sliced your ass?" Milan sarcastically asked. She was halfway dressed by that time.

"Bitch you got five seconds to get out my room and my house, or you're gonna be next. The only difference is I'll slit your throat, you sheisty ass hoe!" I snapped.

Milan giggled as if she took what I was saying for a joke and gave me a dismissive wave of her hand. I charged at her as she was trying to put the rest of her clothes on and Chief stopped me dead in my tracks.

"You need to calm down before you hurt my baby," Chief tried to reason with me.

"You weren't thinking about hurting your baby before were you? If you were you wouldn't have put our child in a situation to be born into some bullshit like this. The baby ain't even here yet and already I'm a single mother!" I shouted.

"Hold up now. One thing I won't allow you to do is keep my child away from me. The baby doesn't have anything to do with what we have going on. So you can kill that single mother talk. We're both adults with understanding. We can discuss this," he reasoned.

"Understanding? Yeah, I *understand* that you been fucking my daughter. What I need for you to understand is that you need to leave," I demanded.

Chief grabbed my hand and pulled me close to him again. He calmly whispered in my ear, "Let me explain myself. You're not even giving me a chance to talk. Please just give me a chance! You know I never meant to hurt you, baby. I didn't want you to find out like this." The words that left his mouth lacked genuineness, and in my heart I knew it wasn't real. In my heart I knew that had I not caught them, it probably would have been a never–ending fling.

"You fuckin' perv!" I screamed so loud, I almost scared my damn self. "I'm pregnant by you and I come home to find you committing adultery with my *daughter*. What do you mean you didn't want me to find out like this? How else would I have found out if I didn't see the shit with my own two eyes? I wouldn't have ever found out because you weren't gonna say shit, and I know that triflin' hoe ass bitch over there wasn't gonna tell me either. You actually think that we 'bout to sit here like some big happy family and talk about something? Nigga, you got me fucked up. It ain't nothing to talk about. I'll have the divorce papers sent to your lawyer by Monday morning. Once the baby gets here, we can discuss visitation or take it to court! Get the fuck out! *Now!*" I snapped. I gave him a look that let him know that I was disgusted with his ass and he better stay the hell away from me.

"I'm not leaving until you talk to me. At least try to work this out with me," he tried to bargain, looking like something out of a horror movie with that big ass open cut leaking blood. He looked hideous and it was all my fault.

"What part about get the fuck out my house don't you understand? I don't know why you are still standing in my face acting like this can be fixed when we both know damn well ain't no coming back from this. If you can fuck my *daughter*, I could never trust you again. Every day I would look at you like the disgusting, filthy, piece of shit that you are. The only thing I regret is getting married and getting pregnant by you. What I won't regret is what I will do to you if you don't leave my fuckin' crib right now. Get going and take that trick ass bitch with you!"

"I'll be that trick ass bitch, but ya husband be lovin' it. That's probably why he's been fuckin' me for two long years. Ain't that right, Chief? Tell her how long you been dickin' me down," she smirked.

I saw Chief look at Milan with the devil in his eyes. Next thing I knew I had my hands around her throat trying to crush her windpipe.

"No this bitch did not just say two years. This shit been going on behind my back for *two years*? So y'all motherfuckers been clocking my ass and working around my schedule so I wouldn't catch y'all, huh?"

My pressure was building and my grip was getting tighter around Milan's neck. I didn't believe what I had heard. I didn't want to believe that I was that fuckin' dumb and blind that I didn't even realize my husband was cheating. I was overwhelmed with emotions and fighting back tears was becoming an impossible task. I wanted to break down right then and there, but I didn't have any plans on letting Milan's throat go. While Chief was trying to pry my fingers from around Milan's throat, her twin sister, London, walked in the room dressed like she had just came from the club.

"What the hell is going on in here?" London wore a confused look on her face "Mama, stop! You're about to kill my sister!"

I let go of Milan's throat when I realized that I was on the verge of killing her. "Why don't you ask your sister?"

London looked at Milan, who was gasping for air, then looked at Chief. She frowned when she saw that Chief's face was split to the white meat.

"Somebody needs to explain what the hell is going on," London demanded.

Chief was at a loss for words as he looked around the room to avoid London's gaze. Milan finally tried to leave the room, but London grabbed her wrist as she was walking out the door and pulled her back in.

"Not until somebody lets me know what's up," London declared.

"Well, since no one has anything to say now I guess I will be the one to let everybody know the truth about y'all disgusting bastards. London, your twin and your step daddy have been having a secret affair for the past two years. You wouldn't happen to have known anything about this, would you?" I eyed my other daughter suspiciously. I didn't know who to trust.

"Hell no I didn't know about that sick shit! You filthy little bitch!! You've been fucking your damn step daddy in our mama's bed!" London came up out of her six inch heels within a matter of seconds and lunged at Milan.

The two of them were going at it like championship boxers until Chief pulled them apart. London then channeled her rage toward Chief when she picked up a brand new crystal vase filled with a dozen white roses and threw it directly at him. He moved just in time for it to miss his head, but it broke on his shoulder. "Bitch ass nigga!" she said, as she threw it.

The black shirt that he was using to cover the gash on his face was soaked with blood but I could see the look in his eyes turn into one of a cold blooded killer. He made a quick move like he was about to go for my daughter and ya'll know I wasn't having that. I jumped on his ass and sunk my teeth into his neck like a vampire thirsting for blood. I tried to bite a plug out his neck. I didn't play when it came to my kids, and everybody that knew me was aware of that, especially Chief.

London came running up on him with the big ass kitchen knife that I kept tucked under the mattress on my side of the bed. At the same time, Milan used whatever strength she had left and in an effort to protect Chief, she grabbed London's wrist and struggled to get the knife from her. For a minute I just sat back and watched the whole thing play out until London smacked fire from Milan, causing her to release the grip she had on London's wrist.

As Milan let go of London's hand and grabbed her face, Chief was able to easily retrieve the knife from London's hand. "Ya'll bitches better chill or it's gonna be a crime scene up in this bitch," he hissed.

The sound of his voice made me cringe because I knew from the way he said it that he damn sure meant it. His whole demeanor changed after London got involved.

Out of nowhere I heard my baby girl, Tiana, speak. "You gotta be quicker than that motherfucker. If it's going to be a crime scene, you're gonna be the one that they're cleaning up off the floor."

All of the chaos came to an abrupt end when the three of us looked back to see that Tiana was aiming a gun directly at Chief. If nothing else could stop Milan from running her mouth before, the sight of her baby sister with that gun damn sure did. She was quiet as a church mouse and she looked like she was scared for her own life. Chief had a look of shock on his face, and I was in complete disbelief. I had no idea that my daughter owned a gun, let alone knew how to use one.

"Where the hell did you get a gun from and why do you have it in your mother's house?" London questioned Tiana, taking the words right out of my mouth.

Tiana completely ignored London and kept her focus on Chief as if no one else was in the room.

"What's the matter, Chief? Cat got your tongue? What was that shit I just heard you talking? Tiana smirked.

"Oh so you a gangsta now, huh? You think you're bad 'cause you got a gun in your hand? Don't be stupid, Tiana. You know what you're doing ain't smart. Put the gun down and I'll forget that any of this ever happened."

No this motherfucker didn't say he'll *forget any of this happened*, I thought.

"No. What's stupid is you bringing a knife to a gun fight." Tiana paused and looked at the knife that Chief had just taken from London. "I don't claim to be a gangster, but I won't hesitate to take an OG out of the game," Tiana countered cockily, with no fear in her eyes.

"Okay, shit is getting too real now! Chief get out of my house and take your mistress with you. Tiana, give me the gun," I pleaded with her.

Milan was still frozen in fear and didn't know what to do.

Tiana never stopped aiming the gun at Chief no matter how much I begged her to give it to me. I had never seen my daughter like that before. It was like she was possessed.

I saw Chief coming towards us and then I heard a bullet break the sound barrier followed by the loud, explosive sound of the shot. I could see the sparks fly from her busting that one shot and she just stood there with a smoking gun in her hand.

CHAPTER 2

Silina

Milan was screaming at the top of her lungs and wailing from the depths of her soul when she saw Chief drop to the floor. London covered her ears and jumped from the loud noise but the sound seemed to have more of an affect her on than the actual shooting.

"Oh my goodness! Tiana, what did you do?" I screamed in a panic.

Tiana started screaming and crying hysterically while she ran out of my room, gun still in hand. I didn't know whether to chase her down and try to console her or help my soon to be ex–husband, so I just stood there in a state of shock.

London saw Milan going to Chief's aid and put a stop to that. "You've done enough disrespectful shit today. You're not about to be up in here grieving. It's time for you to go!"

"What about Chief?" Milan cried.

As the tears freely fell down my cheeks, Chief looked at me like he was begging for me to help him. I couldn't feel sorry for that sick bastard even if I wanted to. The pain he had caused me was worse than any bullet could ever be. If he was lucky, he would eventually be put out of his misery. I had to live with the pain of knowing that my daughter and husband slash baby daddy had carried on a secret affair right under my nose forever. My mind was telling me to help him, but my heart wanted him to endure the same agony that I felt.

When Milan hadn't budged from her spot, London helped her out by grabbing her by her arm and pulling her toward the stairs. Milan tried to put up a fight when London started pulling and grabbing on her. She placed her feet firmly on the floor in an attempt to avoid getting dragged. The only thing that did was make London get rougher with her.

"Bitch, let's go!" London snapped, pulling her even harder.

"What am I supposed to do? Y'all know I ain't got nowhere to go," she cried, realizing how fucking stupid she was for doing any of this.

"I don't give a damn what you do. I know what you won't be doing and that's spending another second in my house. From here on out you are dead to this family. Just looking at your face is making me sick to my stomach. You don't deserve to be in my presence. You were a waste of a sperm," I announced, as I descended the stairs behind them. I didn't even try to stop London from man handling her sister. Her ass was lucky I wasn't the one doing it. They both looked up at me as I spoke. "I always made sure you were well taken care of, but you burned that bridge when you decided you wanted to open your legs to my husband. I know I always taught you to never bite the hand that feeds you."

London butted in with her two cents. "Yeah, that sounds like a personal problem to me, but you heard what my mama

25

said. Get out of her house! Bring your ass on now, bitch!" She opened the front door and motioned for Milan to get out.

When Milan didn't move quickly enough, London tried to push her out of the door. Milan tried to get her sister's hands off her and made an attempt to fight back. There weren't too many that could stand a chance against London. She would fight dudes and give them a run for their money, so fighting Milan was like taking candy from a baby to her.

"Wait a minute bitch; I don't give a fuck what you say. I'm not leaving here without my shit!" Milan got the strength to push her way back through the door and it swung open so hard that it knocked London to the floor.

Milan took that time to rush past us and go in the coat closet and retrieve her purse and a coat. There was also a pair of sneakers in there that she slid on her feet without any socks. I didn't even try to stop her because I was not up for fighting anymore, I just wanted her gone. After I helped London off the floor she tried to get at Milan again but I held her back. She

26

wasn't even worth any more of our energy. Once Milan threw

the pea coat on with just her bra underneath she stormed out of

the house with her nose up in the air.

"I called Uncle Tony so he can help us figure out what to

do next," Tiana said to me as she was coming down the stairs.

She was still hysterically crying.

"You got some explaining to do, Tiana. But I don't have

the time or energy to do it right now," I sighed. "We need to

call the police and get this man out of my house!"

"Nooo!" You can't call the police! Don't you know that

they will lock me up and throw away the key? If I hadn't shot

him, there's no telling what he would have done to us!"

"So what are we supposed to do just let him die? As much

as I hate his life I don't want his blood on my hands."

"Let's just wait until Uncle Tony gets here and see what he

thinks we should do. I already lost one sister, I'm not trying to

lose both in one night," London tried to reason with me.

"Y'all have lost your damn minds! This is too much bullshit for one night! I wish I would have just kept my ass in Florida!" I vented.

My daughters looked at me with pity in their eyes, but they didn't say a word.

Tiana was the one to break the silence. "Mama please, don't call the police."

I shook my head and ran back up the stairs to my bedroom. To my surprise, Chief wasn't even dead. His ass was squirming around on the floor like the snake. He was trying to get to his phone, leaving a blood trail all over my freshly waxed hardwood floor. At that moment something came over me, almost like I was possessed. There was no compassion in my heart for him. I wasn't about to let his ass call for help. I would have rather watched his ass croak. I wanted him to go through the same pain and suffering that he had put me through. He wasn't the only one that was experiencing what it was like to be near death. Little did he know I was dying a slow, agonizing death on the inside.

My imagination ran wild with the possibilities of what had really gone down with him and Milan over the past two years. I wondered if he touched her the same way he touched me, treated her the way he had treated me, and loved her the way he had claimed to have loved me. Those thoughts were enough to drive me insane.

Chief looked me in my eyes. He struggled and said, "I still love you, Silina. I always will."

The expression on his face told me that he meant what he'd just said, but then again he could have just wanted me to call somebody that could save his ass. He probably thought he was about to die and knew that he was the one who had fucked up and brought all this shit upon himself. I couldn't trust or believe a damn thing that he said.

"Till death do us part," I whispered viciously in his ear. "Who would have thought that death would come so soon?" I asked him rhetorically, before I stood up and left the room.

I knew I had lost my damn mind when I was watching my husband stare into the face of death and I didn't give a damn. The only thing I felt was rage, and I wanted him to suffer like I was suffering. I didn't even recognize the woman that I was at that moment. I completely understood what happens to those women on *Snapped* when they snapped and killed their husbands. It was like the rage took control and I had no control over my own actions. I guess that was what they considered a crime of passion.

I went downstairs to sit in my special room, so I could get my thoughts together…or at least *try* to. My special room was actually a den that I got renovated and had French doors added to the entrance, so that it could be my own personal space. I had a beautiful winter white chaise lounge right in the center of the room. That was the only piece of furniture I needed.

My room was for me and me only, and I made sure that everyone got the hint. I got white, fluffy carpet added from wall to wall, just in that room. When the sunshine came in through the humongous window that extended from the ceiling to the floor, mixed with all that white, the room almost appeared heavenly. To top it off, I had my walls painted sky blue with beautiful white clouds on every wall. The ceiling was a midnight blue, and it had stars covering it. In a sense, being in that room made me feel closer to God.

As soon as I stepped into the room, I sat down on the chair and instantly started crying. I was hurting to the core. I didn't know how I was going to get over the mess that Chief and Milan had caused in our lives. People always knew me to be a strong woman, but I damn sure didn't feel like one. I started questioning myself in my mind, wondering if I had done something wrong or why I wasn't able to keep him happy. If that had been the case, he should have just told me he wasn't happy instead of fucking my damn daughter. I was crying so hard I felt myself about to have a panic attack. My nose was running and my face was drenched with tears. Between crying and sniffling, it was hard for me to even breathe. The cramping I had been feeling in my belly was getting hard to ignore. I knew I was a mess. I was going through too many emotions at once, and this pregnancy wasn't making it any better.

I sighed heavily as my beautiful girls entered the room and came and sat down with me. Tiana was shaking like a leaf on a tree and she hadn't stopped crying yet. London seemed indifferent about the situation, like it didn't bother her one way or another. Even though London and Milan were twins, Tiana didn't look much different from them. As a matter of fact, they were all the spitting image of me. All three of them had my flawless honey brown skin tone, and my thick jet black hair. They all had big beautiful brown eyes with long eyelashes. But the looks were where the similarities ended because they all had their own unique personalities.

London had her hair cut into a bob, one side hanging to her shoulder and the other side cut right to her chin, with the back cut shorter. She had blonde highlights throughout her feathered side bang. Milan kept her hair jet black and always wore a blow out that fell down her back and stopped at her chest in the front. Tiana's hair was the longest, and she usually had hers up in a messy bun. She wasn't really the girly girl type like her sisters, but she was a natural beauty. Her face was lightly splashed with little brown freckles and she had two deep dimples that resembled craters in both her cheeks. The twins were identical, but London had a distinguishable beauty mark on the left side of her nose. London and Tiana were slim like me, but Milan was thick. She had thick thighs and a round, voluptuous ass that could make a grown man cry. She had the curvy hips and small waist to go along with it. And she had some perky C cup tits. I couldn't lie. My daughter had it going on. She looked like she could be one of them video bitches.

I was proud of the two girls that were sitting here with me. They had grown up to be the strong, intelligent women I raised them to be. They kept all the morals and values I had instilled in them. London had graduated from Hampton University's School of Pharmacy with a bachelor's degree in pharmaceutical sales, and she was currently in grad school majoring in pharmacology. Tiana was in her sophomore year at Norfolk State University, and she was going to be a computer information systems manager. My girls had goals and they wanted a lot out of life, so they were putting in the work to get what they wanted. I always taught them to have a boss mentality, and that nothing was ever going to get handed to them. Milan on the other hand, decided to go left instead of right, I guess.

I will be the first to admit that I spoiled my girls because I wanted them to have everything that I didn't. I also taught them that you had to work for what you wanted. I rewarded them for good behavior, excellent grades, and many other things that they did to make me proud. They knew that if they kept up the good work, they would always get rewarded for it. That never seemed to register to Milan. It was my fault because in all actuality, I spoiled Milan more than her sisters. London and Tiana deserved everything they got, but I always felt bad about leaving Milan out, so I could never do it. I never wanted my children to think any one of them was getting more special treatment than the other. It didn't take Milan long to catch on to the fact that she didn't have to do anything and she was still getting everything she wanted. Her ass never cleaned up a damn thing and her grades in high school were terrible. Hell, her ass barely graduated high school. Milan had a smart ass mouth that I constantly had to get on her about. She basically did whatever the fuck she wanted to do. She never listened to anything anyone told her. She became an attention whore, always trying to steal the spotlight from her sisters and make everything about her. I guess it was the fact that she was a middle child and a twin. She made sure that she stood out more than her sisters did, and most of the time she used her looks and body to do that instead of her brain. I should have seen this shit coming from a mile away.

I started to wonder what to do next. I wasn't expecting for everything to go that far, and I had no idea that my baby girl would actually shoot a man. I knew that I couldn't get the police involved. I would rather for him to die than for my daughter to go to jail. I looked over at my baby girl who had just lost her innocence. I don't even think *she* had expected it to go that far. She was in the most fragile state I had ever seen her in.

The doorbell rang and snapped me out of my thoughts.

"That must be Uncle Tony," London said.

I had completely forgotten that my brother was even on his way. We all headed to the front door, to let Tony in the house. We needed him to help us figure out what to do. He was the right person to call for something like this. When we were kids, our grandma, who'd raised us after our mom committed suicide, struggled with the two of us. She was too old to work and she had a slew of medical issues. Her Social Security benefits were barely enough to cover the rent and bills. We barely had food to eat at times. My brother, Tony, went to the streets and did whatever he had to do to feed us. He robbed grocery stores just to get food. He jacked drug dealers for their packs and learned how to hustle at a very early age.

The streets sucked him in. And even at the age of forty–three, he was still knee deep in the game. The only thing that had changed was his street smarts. He had the mind and the resources to handle situations just like the one we were in. When Tony came into the house, he didn't say a word. He headed straight upstairs to the master bedroom. I guess Tiana had already said enough over the phone. Something seemed strange though because he only stayed in the room for a couple of seconds before returning with a puzzled look on his face.

"I thought that you said that Chief got shot and he was dying as we spoke," Tony said, scratching his long locks like he always did when he was confused.

"What's wrong?" I asked him.

"Chief is gone," he responded.

"Gone…like *dead*, right?" I asked.

"If he is, he damn sure didn't die here." Tony answered.

I almost broke my neck running up the stairs to see what the hell Tony was talking about. When I made it to my bedroom and saw what he was talking about, I let out a deep gasp.

"No fucking way!" I was surprised to find that Chief may be still alive and his ass was gone! The only sign of him was an enormous trail of blood going from the floor all the way to the window. I knew that motherfucker didn't get out of the damn window by himself. I wondered who had helped him. Then I remembered leaving his cell phone within reach when I ran downstairs. It was gone now too!

I ran over to the window and there was no sign of him anywhere. But what I did see was a ladder right under my window. It was like someone left in a hurry and didn't have time to grab the ladder. It took someone with skills to climb up a ladder, enter the room, lift Chief, and drag his big ass down the

ladder. They'd done it without being seen or heard. I had

obviously underestimated Chief.

"What's going on? Ya'll are scaring me," London said. She

stopped dead in her tracks. "That's impossible," she whispered,

while she stood there frozen in shock.

"He's gone."

CHAPTER 3

Milan

"Daddy no...please stop it. I don't want to do this again tonight. You're hurting me, Daddy. I'm telling Mommy," I said through sobs and tear filled eyes, trembling in terror watching my father as he approached my bed.

He had that look in his eyes that let me know that the inevitable was going to happen no matter how hard I cried and begged him not to. I was only ten years old when my daddy started raping me. I never told anyone because he threatened to kill my mom and my sisters if I said a word. At such a young age, I never wanted anybody to hurt my family. I figured that if he killed them I would be left all alone with him forever. There was no way I could endure that type of torture for the rest of my life.

He looked me in my eyes and moved my hair which was stuck to my face from all the tears. He started to kiss me on my forehead like I was the most precious child in the world. I kicked my feet in an effort to stop him from going any further, but he still managed to snatch my legs open and rip my panties off me. He took two fingers with dirty fingernails inside my kitty and started to curl them in a 'come here' motion. The next thing I knew, he was pulling out his private part and ramming it inside of me with no remorse. He put a pillow over my face to block out my screams.

"If you don't shut the fuck up right now I'm going to blow your mama's brains out," he whispered in an intimidating voice. The way I saw him beat on my mommy every day, I believed his threat.

My insides were on fire as I felt him pumping in and out of me, ripping me apart. I couldn't breathe because of the pillow that was smothering me, so I started clawing at his back and trying my hardest to fight for some air. The harder I fought the more he pressed down on the pillow. I prayed that somebody would come and help me, but I knew it wouldn't happen. After a few more minutes of torture, he started shooting a warm, sticky liquid all over the inside of my leg. He took a hot rag and wiped me clean before he disappeared out of the room as if nothing had just happened. This had been a regular routine for me for four years, practically every night until he got locked up. The sad thing about it was, nobody had ever noticed.

My phone vibrating snapped me out of the vivid thoughts of my past. I looked at the caller ID and saw that it was Tiana calling me again. I hadn't talked to her since she had shot Chief a few weeks ago and I didn't plan on talking to her any time soon. She was probably shitting bricks, wondering if I was going to rat her out to the boys. I didn't plan on going to the cops then, but I was damn sure going to keep it in mind just in case I ever needed "insurance". I hit ignore and put the phone back down on the table.

It wasn't easy for me to get past Chief getting shot. Watching somebody get shot in front of you was a traumatic experience no matter who the person was. But I had dealt with it like I'd dealt with all my other demons. I couldn't stop thinking about the way that entire scenario had played out. I didn't think that our little secret would end up getting him killed.

Our little fling had started back when Chief asked me to be the one to meet up with his cocaine connect up in Maryland. I was down for it because I'd always been all about the money. He had offered to pay me $5,000 for each trip. Needless to say, I started taking that trip for him just about every week. At first, I was paranoid as hell, driving back to Virginia with ten bricks of coke in my trunk, but when that money started rolling in, I stopped caring. I got addicted to the fast money and I was going to get it by any means.

I went on more shopping sprees and vacations than you could imagine and I didn't even look at price tags. London's nosy ass used to ask me if I was trickin' because she didn't know where all that money was coming from. Everybody was looking at me sideways because they knew damn well I didn't have a job, but I always had stacks of money to blow. If they wanted to think I was trickin' then that was exactly what I let them believe.

I was the one who came on to Chief first. He turned me down the first couple of times, but of course he eventually gave in to temptation. It just so happened that his sex game was better than I expected and we kept coming back for more. To me it was the perfect opportunity to make my mother feel my pain. My own father had taken advantage of me for years, and she didn't even bother to find out what was wrong with me. I never told her what was going on because I was ashamed. I felt disgusted and humiliated and I doubted that anyone would ever believe me. My sisters were the last people I wanted to confide in because I didn't believe they were getting the same treatment.

I hated everything about my father. I was getting sexually assaulted and my mother was nowhere to be found. When I needed her the most, she preferred to work around the clock to stay away from the house as much as possible. She was never at home, so she didn't notice that her daughter was no longer an innocent little girl. I couldn't blame my mom for not wanting to be around because I had watched her take many ass whippings. My father would get drunk and beat her senseless. In exchange for her lack of time spent with us, she spoiled us with gifts. We always wore the flyest clothes, shoes, and bling. We could ask for pretty much anything we wanted and expect to get it. But that materialistic shit wasn't what I needed then. It didn't make up for her lack of protection from the evils of the world like a mother was supposed to provide.

When I entered my pre–teen years, I started running away from home. I was constantly suspended from school for fighting. Any little thing somebody said or did would piss me off and I wouldn't hesitate to fuck somebody up. I even picked fights with my sisters and became disrespectful toward my mom. Nobody ever wondered why I hated to be in my father's presence or why I never said a word to him. Everybody always thought I was just trying to be grown. I didn't understand why no one could see that I was miserable in my own skin. I was young and confused. With no one to turn to, it didn't take long for my heart to turn as cold as ice. Little did Silina know I harbored a lot of resentment towards her.

I decided that I wasn't about to waste any more time thinking about my family. I got my revenge and they were just as dead to me as I was to them. I didn't have anything against Tiana personally. I just chose not to deal with her.

"I need to get back to figuring out how to get my money back up," I said to myself.

The night I got kicked to the curb I stayed in a hotel. Those heifers were tripping if they thought I was leaving that house without my purse and my car keys. Luckily for me I was smart enough to have stashed some of that money I had made working for Chief. I had accumulated $150,000 in my savings account. That was nothing compared to all the money I had blown through, but it was good enough for the time being. I was out of that hotel within three days because I went and rented a condo in downtown Norfolk. I paid the rent up for a year so that would be one less thing I had to worry about. I didn't take anything from my mother's house except my car, so I had to buy brand new everything. I made sure I hooked my crib up and bought myself a whole new wardrobe. I was living comfortably for the moment, but I knew the money was going to run out soon, especially considering the way I liked to splurge.

I knew that getting a job was out of the question for me. I had never worked a 9 to 5 a day in my life, and I damn sure didn't want to start now. I went from getting whatever I wanted from my mom to making a large amount of money on my own without having to do shit. I wanted it to stay that way.

What can I do to maintain the lifestyle I've grown accustomed to?

For a second the thought of hopping on somebody's pole crossed my mind, but I quickly dismissed the idea. I wasn't *that* desperate. Besides, I knew damn well strippers in Virginia were barely pulling in any bread. Being degraded for a few dollars was definitely not the move.

Suddenly, the idea of using the money that I had left to buy a brick of that cocaine hit me. I knew where I could find Chief's connect, so getting it wasn't the problem. The only issue I had to iron out was who the hell I would sell it to. I wouldn't know where to start or even who to deal with. Then I remembered that the possibility of finding a crack head in Norfolk was the same as finding a clown in a circus. You couldn't go out there and not expect to see at least one.

Knowing the type of money Chief was pulling in made me want to put my plan into effect. Realizing I didn't know shit about selling the drug, cooking it, or even how to bag it up hindered my plans once again.

"Maybe I'll just find the dealers and get them to spend their money with me. I'll get it for cheap and give them a price that they can't refuse. That way I won't have to actually get my hands dirty, but I'll still be coming up in the game." A slick smile spread across my face when I thought about all the money I was about to be making.

It was settled in my mind. I was going to take that trip to Maryland.

CHAPTER 4

Milan

I pulled up to the back of the restaurant in Bethesda, Maryland where I always did my exchange. I was looking good and feeling good because my bruise covered face had completely healed. I was back! I was dressed in all black, rocking a pair of leather Balmain jeans, a tight fitted cardigan, and a pair of Giuseppe Zanotti wedge sneakers. My look was topped off with a pea coat, scarf, and leather gloves. My fresh blow out flowed down my back and I rocked a part down the middle.

The owner of the restaurant was a notorious king pin who had started his business with drug money. We had it set up where I would enter a secret back door that only a few people knew about. It led to some basement or some shit underground and he had an office down there too. It was soundproof, so that the people in the restaurant couldn't hear what was really going on.

I strutted down the hall that led to the office with confidence in every step. The ugly black ass nigga that always guarded the office was standing outside the door eyeballing me like he wanted to eat me. He was fat as hell and the way he was looking at my body made me feel uncomfortable.

When I walked up to him, I handed him the bag of money like I usually did with Chief's money. We never said a word to each other for as long as I had been going there. This time, when I went to give him the money he started to open the office door.

"The boss wants to see you. He's been expecting you," the man said, in a raspy voice.

As many times as I had been there, I'd only seen this big time hustler a couple of times in passing. Apparently, he had a flunkie that did his dirty work while he collected all the money.

"Don't just stand there; get your ass in there. He ain't got all day," the man snapped.

I rolled my eyes at him and flicked his ass off before I walked in. I didn't know who the fuck he thought he was talking to. When I entered the office, I saw the finest motherfucker I'd ever laid eyes on. He had milk chocolate skin and he was sporting a low cut along with a freshly trimmed beard and mustache. He kind of reminded me of Morris Chestnut. You could tell that he took very good care of himself. He wore a diamond in each ear and a gold and diamond pinky ring. He was also rocking an expensive diamond splattered watch. To say the least, the man looked like money.

The inside of the office was huge, but the odd thing that caught my attention the more than anything was the massive book case that stretched across his entire back wall. It had to be about six feet tall and every inch of it was filled with books. He had a damn library in his office. He also had a mini refrigerator and a fish tank that held exotic fish. There were TV screens with a view of every angle of the restaurant on each screen. The décor in there was beautiful with unique pieces of art gracing the walls. Either he had a wonderful sense of style or he had a woman with one. I had to admit I was very impressed and I wasn't easily impressed.

For a moment, he just stared at me with a blank expression on his face. I couldn't tell what the hell was on his mind.

"You wanted to see me?" I asked, breaking the uncomfortable silence.

"Yeah, I did. You can relax though. You're over there looking like you just got called down to the principal's office. You look nervous as hell, Milan. You can chill out. I promise I won't call your parents," he joked.

"What? Who said anything about me being nervous and how do you know my name?" I asked suspiciously.

"It wouldn't take a rocket scientist to figure it out. I usually don't listen to what comes out of other people's mouths because most of the time it's bullshit, so I pay more attention to their actions. I know you're gonna say you ain't nervous, but you standing over there fiddling with your hands and you haven't made eye contact with me yet." He paused and looked up at me like he was waiting for me to look him in his eyes.

I instantly shut his little theory down by staring him dead in his face. Nobody made me nervous anymore, and I wasn't about to let him think he did.

"You must not be as smart as I thought you were," he said.

"Come again?" I had to make sure I had heard that motherfucker right because I knew damn well he did not just insult my intelligence.

"You asked me how I knew your name. You didn't actually think that you were coming in and out of here without me knowing who you were, did you? That would be as dumb as you letting a complete stranger do business in your house without you knowing shit about them. If I were that careless, somebody would have already tried to take me out and get what's mine. I know everybody that steps foot in my territory. I know more about them than they know about me. So if anybody ever tries to fuck me over I know exactly where to find them and they won't see me coming."

The way he had said those words was almost as if he was issuing a warning.

I didn't know how to take what he had just said. Was he telling me that he had been watching me?

"Oh, so you're stalking me now?" I asked. "Next time you want to say something to me, make sure you choose your words wisely. Don't ever try to insult my intelligence."

He smirked like what I'd said amused him. "I never said that you're not intelligent. All I was saying was you couldn't have thought that question all the way through before you asked it. Anybody that has any type of common sense would have already known the answer to that."

"So now I don't have any common sense? I think you need to just stop talking and get to the point of why you called me in here."

Even though I didn't admit it to him I could tell that he was a smart man. Staying one step ahead of the game was always important. He didn't respond to me right away. He looked like he was checking me out which was typical of most men. Not a day went by that I didn't become some man's fantasy.

The more I looked at him the sexier he became. I caught myself staring at him and I didn't even care if he noticed. His beautiful chocolate skin made me want to eat him up like a Hershey's kiss. It was so smooth and so flawless with no blemishes in sight. He had the prettiest set of white teeth I had ever seen next to my million dollar smile. I could see how big his chest was through his shirt and my mind couldn't help but imagine what his bare chest looked like. I pictured myself rubbing my hands all over that chiseled body of his. I didn't notice how long I was fantasizing about him until he snapped me out of my thoughts.

"I know I look good. But unless you're gonna let me know what's going through your mind, you shouldn't be undressing me with your eyes like that." He gave me a seductive grin and winked his eye at me.

"You caught me," I smirked. "You ain't low either. I can only imagine what you were thinking about doing to me.

"Maybe one day you can find out. How about we start with me taking you out and getting to know a little bit more about you." He smiled, flashing those pearly whites again.

"I would love to take you up on that offer, but I've heard that nothing good comes from mixing business and pleasure."

"That may be true, but I don't plan on doing any more business with you. I don't think you're fit for the game and I can't take any chances with my empire. There's no room for any weak links. The weak link will be the one to break under pressure and I can't afford that," he stated.

"What makes you think that I'm a weak link? You don't even know me, so how can you tell me what I'm fit for?"

"How far would you be willing to go if somebody else's freedom or life was on the line? Can you be trusted not to snitch on anybody when you get in that room and they start applying pressure? Are you willing to kill or be killed? That's what you have to do to survive out here. When you're in this game you never know who's plotting against you, so you have to stay prepared. The most important question you need to ask yourself is: Are you willing to lose your life for some fast money?"

He looked at me like he was waiting for a reply, but I didn't say a word. I hadn't even thought about all the risks and dangers. All I had ever seen was the glamorous side to drug money. I was never exposed to any of the dirt that happened on a regular. I knew I wasn't about that jail life. I was not about to be sitting in a cell with other women with bad hygiene for one day, let alone for years. As much as I loved money, I wasn't willing to die for it. There had to be some other way.

"That's exactly what I thought," he said, breaking the silence. "I'm just trying to stop you from getting into some shit you ain't ready for."

"I didn't take this trip to Maryland for nothing, though. So at least just let me have my last run. Nothing has happened to me in all this time, so one more flip can't possibly hurt." I tried to reason with him. I figured if I at least doubled my money I would be okay for a little while until I came up with a new plan.

"Did you hear what I just said? I won't allow you to leave here with drugs. If anything were to happen to you in that *last run*. I would feel guilty for giving it to you. Plus I don't know if I can trust you not to tell on me just yet, but I plan on finding out. Do you have any plans for tonight?"

"My plan was to get back home and get my money rolling, but I guess that won't be happening," I said sarcastically.

"Well, how about you roll with me? I'll show you a good time and make you forget all about the money."

"I highly doubt that you will be able to take my mind off of money, but I'm down with having some fun tonight."

I decided that it wouldn't hurt to go out with him and see what he was about. I figured I could talk him into letting me flip my money. I wasn't going to give up that easily because I was on a paper chase. I had my way of manipulating men, or anybody for that matter, into giving me what I wanted. He wouldn't be any different.

When he stood up I noticed how tall he was. He was about 6'2" and as he stood over me I inhaled his captivating scent. He was wearing Yves Saint Laurent cologne.

He even smells like money.

We walked out of the office and exited the building. Once we stopped in front of a navy blue Camaro, he opened the passenger door for me to get in.

"I'll just follow you in my car. I can't just leave my car here. For all I know, you could be crazy, and I don't trust a soul. I'll feel better knowing that I can leave whenever I want to. Besides, I don't even know your name," I said.

"I won't argue with you on that. Do what you want to do. I just hope you can keep up. By the way, you can call me Elijah."

"You don't have to worry about me keeping up. I got this."

When I got in my black Audi, and he got in his Camaro, we took off. We weren't driving for long before we pulled up in front of Ruth Chris Steak House on Wisconsin Avenue. We both parked our cars in the parking garage and made our way into the restaurant.

The set up of the restaurant was beautiful. There were marble floors and cherry wood tables and chairs. From the bar that sat in the middle of the restaurant, you could see an amazing view of the city from the huge windows. I loved the ambience of the place, and I was impressed with Elijah's pick for our date.

The blond, blue eyed hostess led us to a table for two. It was the middle of the afternoon, so the restaurant wasn't that crowded. Fortunately, we had just missed the lunch rush and we beat the people that would come in for dinner. Elijah helped me take off my coat, draped it over the back of my chair, and pulled the chair out for me to sit down.

"Can I start you off with something to drink?" the hostess asked us while handing us menus.

"Let us get a bottle of Pinot Noir, Au Contraire," Elijah spoke up.

"I'll get that to you right away, and your waiter will be with you shortly," she said with a smile.

Not even a minute later the hostess returned with the red wine and two wine glasses. She poured it into the glasses for us and told us to enjoy our meal before she walked off.

I took a sip of the smooth wine before I started talking. "So what made you decide that you wanted to take me out?"

He swallowed damn near the whole glass of wine in one gulp while looking me intensely in my eyes. "I'm attracted to you. You're a beautiful woman and I like your style. I want to know more about you, so I decided to ask you out, that's all, ma."

He gazed deeply into my eyes, but I broke the stare because I didn't like what it was doing to me. I liked to remain in control at all times, but something about this man had me thinking about cooking and cleaning for his ass. He was so intriguing and fine as hell.

"My name is Frank and I'll be serving you today. Have you decided what you'll be having?"

"You want me to order for you?" Elijah asked me.

"I guess I can see what kind of taste you have," I smiled seductively.

"We'll both have the petite filet and shrimp entrée. I'll take mashed potatoes and broccoli au gratin on the side," he handed our menus back to the waiter.

"I will get that out to you as soon as possible. Let me know if you need anything else."

Our conversation started back up as soon as the waiter was out of earshot.

"What makes a lady like you want to get involved in the streets?"

"I gotta get money some type of way. Working a regular ass job ain't gonna provide me with the type of money I need to maintain my lifestyle. I have to get it how I can, and that was the easiest way I could think of at the time. It beats sliding down somebody's pole for $100," I stated.

Elijah laughed at my last statement. "It does beat that, but I wouldn't even lie and tell you that it's easy. People only see the money, cars, clothes, and hoes when they think of hustlers. But it comes with a lot more bullshit than that. You have to constantly watch your back because somebody is always trying to come up. There are people out here who will rob, steal, and kill for their families and they aren't going to care who you are. You will never really know who you can trust. A lot of people lose their souls to the streets not only because of the shit they have to see, but what they have to do. Like I said to you earlier, sometimes it comes down to you having to kill or be killed. I have watched grown men turn into bitches. I've seen people crack under pressure once they were behind that wall, taking everyone in the operation down with him. You couldn't even imagine half the shit that goes on," Elijah put me on to game. He spoke in a hushed voice so that no one around could hear him.

"Damn, now that you put it like that you got me second guessing my decision to come here."

"If you didn't come here, you wouldn't be sitting right here with me. Everything happens for a reason." He flashed that gorgeous smile of his. I never saw a set of teeth that perfect in my life.

"You're right about that. I'm enjoying myself, so I guess my trip wasn't a complete waste. Let me ask you this. After all the things you just explained to me why are you involved in the streets? You're all telling me all the cons of the game, but you're pushing dope across the east coast."

"The streets are all I know. I was born into this because my father was a hustler. I was exposed to a lot of shit that I shouldn't have seen at such an early age. My dad schooled me on how to always be on top before he got killed." He paused when he mentioned the death of his father. I saw the pain of the tragic loss in his eyes. "When he got shot to death when I was eighteen, I jumped into the streets even more. The only thing that changed was that I got smarter. And that's why I am the successful business man that I am today."

The waiter interrupted our conversation by setting our plates in front of us. Just smelling the food made my mouth water. It looked even more appetizing. I didn't waste any time digging in to the scrumptious, juicy steak topped with jumbo shrimp. We hardly said a word to each other as we devoured the delicious meal.

"I guess I did a smart thing by trusting you to select my entrée. It was delicious," I said when I was on my last few bites. I finished off the rest of my wine and poured myself another glass.

"That's not the only thing you can trust me with. Hopefully, I'll impress you enough tonight to make you want to go on another date with me."

We talked for a little while longer then he paid for our check. We exited the restaurant and started walking toward our cars. The sun was setting in the city, creating a beautiful scene. When we entered the parking garage it was unusually quiet to me. I noticed a black Escalade truck with its motor running, but I didn't pay it much attention. As soon as Elijah went to open my car door for me, the driver of the black truck started firing off shots from the window,

"Get down, Milan!" Elijah shouted as he threw me to the ground positioning my body between two cars.

He pulled a small gun from one of his Timberland boots and started busting back at the shooter in the truck. I was on the ground screaming and covering my head, praying that I wouldn't get shot. I could hear glass being shattered and it was hitting the ground all around me. After a 30 second exchange of gun fire, I heard the tires of the truck screeching as they pulled out of the garage. I lifted my head just in time to see that Elijah shoot two bullets through the windshield. I didn't know if it hit the person or not, but I was glad that I wasn't hurt. I was relieved that Elijah was okay too.

Elijah came and helped me up off the ground and told me to get in the passenger side of my car and let him drive. He left his car right where it was and hauled ass out of the parking lot. He made it out just in time to hear the police sirens coming from a distance.

"What the fuck was that about?" I shouted, angry that I got put in a sticky situation because of him.

"I don't know, but I'm damn sure going to find out. I got a glimpse of somebody's face when they were pulling off. It was the passenger. I know I'm not tripping, that was ya boy *Chief*!"

My heart damn near jumped out of my chest when he said that he'd seen Chief shooting at us. I just knew that he was as good as dead. So many questions ran through my mind at the mention of his name. Did he follow me here? Was he trying to kill me because he blamed me for what happened to him? It had to have been me that he was after, because as far as I knew he never had any problems with Elijah. I knew that my mouth had dug him into a deeper hole than he was already in that night, but I didn't think that was reason enough to kill me. What I did know was that had Elijah not been there, I probably would've been dead.

"I'm sorry you were put in danger like that. You don't have to worry though because you're protected when you're with me. I heard through the grapevine that Chief was on some bullshit. After all this time I've been doing business with him he wanna decide to try to knock out the competition. I didn't want to believe that about him because he had always been loyal to me. See what I mean when I say that you will never know who you can trust? The object of illusion is a motherfucker. I can't believe I almost got caught slipping!"

Hearing what Elijah had said that people were telling him about Chief made a light bulb go off in my head. It was the perfect opportunity for me to get Chief got before he got me.

"Now that you mention it, I did hear Chief discussing some type of takeover before. He was saying something about expanding and moving in on other territories and knocking the competition out. The competition being *you*." I looked at him. I made sure I made every word I said sound believable.

An angry scowl came across Elijah's face and he looked like he was ready to kill. "I'm dropping you off at my condo, so I can go take care of something. I don't want Chief thinking that you turned against the family because I know he saw you with me. Let me make it safe for you to go home first.

We pulled into the parking garage of a high rise building in Bethesda, less than twenty minutes away from the restaurant. We got out of the car and walked into the entrance of the immaculate condominium building. Once we got in the elevator, I could feel the difference in the vibe between me and

70

Elijah. His demeanor went from the perfect gentleman to a cold blooded killer. I could tell by the look in his eyes and the way he was moving that he wasn't going to rest until he finished what Chief had started. We got off the elevator on the 16th floor and walked down the hall. Elijah's condo was the only one on the floor. He unlocked the door for me and motioned for me to step inside, walking in right behind me.

"Make yourself comfortable. Help yourself to whatever you want. If you need to get some rest, there is a guest room on the first floor," he said as he rushed past me and ran up the few stairs that led to a second floor bedroom. He came back out the room with an automatic weapon that he tucked into his waist. "I'll be back." He turned around and walked off like a man on a mission.

Once again I was impressed by his taste. His condo was nice and cozy, decorated with warm, inviting colors. His furniture was tan and he had a burnt orange wooden coffee table on the center of a rug with a big leopard in the middle. He had a few plants strategically placed around the room, some big and some small. Beige curtains adorned the patio door, which showed a beautiful view of the city.

He had an entertainment center that held a sixty inch smart TV, a DVD player, stereo, and surround sound. There were also pictures of him and people that I assumed were his family. The dining room had the same color scheme, with a brown dinette table that seated six. The place mats on the table were crème with gold trim, and on top of them were the finest china dishes. He had to have a personal decorator, because I didn't know any man that had that much sense of style. I flopped down on the couch and made myself comfortable.

I didn't know what was going to happen to Chief that night or if anything would go down at all. I was hoping that Elijah did catch him. I couldn't believe that he clearly saw me and shot at me like I was a nigga off the streets.

You done fucked up now Chief. You don't know that you just started a war. You tried to get me for some reason, and now I'm going to get you.

I sat back with a satisfied grin on my face, knowing that I was about to get revenge on Chief without even having to lift a finger. I had gotten Elijah to play into my hands exactly how I wanted him to.

CHAPTER 5

Silina

HELLO SILINA! I KNOW YOU SEE ME CALLING AND TEXTING YOU. I CAME TO YOUR HOUSE AND SAW YOUR CAR SO I KNOW YOU'RE IN THERE. WHAT THE FUCK IS GOING ON? CALL ME ASAP.

I looked at my phone and ignored yet another text message from my friend, Precious. I knew she was pissed because she was typing in all caps. She was probably worried sick about me, but I wasn't ready to face anybody yet. If I were to talk to her, I would have to tell her what was going on. Having to actually speak about it to someone else made the situation too real for me, and I still hadn't faced reality about it yet. I still woke up hoping that it all was a bad dream. No matter what I did, I couldn't escape the images of walking in on my husband and child doing unspeakable things. It replayed over and over in my mind like a terrible nightmare.

I fell into a depression so deep that I couldn't pull myself out of it. I didn't want to eat and I rarely slept because I couldn't close my eyes without seeing Chief laying on the floor bleeding. I didn't answer any phone calls or text messages from anyone. Precious went as far as coming to my house and knocking on the door, but I left her standing on the porch. I was glad I had a good friend like her that I could trust to run my business without me around. I wasn't even worried about my boutique going under because I knew she had everything under control.

My daughters were worried about me. I knew it killed them to see me like this, but they let me grieve in my own way. They did check on me around the clock and took turns making sure someone was home with me at all times. They were probably worried about me doing something stupid like killing myself, but I wasn't that far gone. What I did know was I had to do something to get out of the funk I was in.

I'M COMING OVER AND YOU BETTER OPEN UP OR I'M BUSTING IN. NOT UP FOR DEBATE!

Precious sent another text message after I didn't respond to the first one. I decided to stop trying to avoid her and let her come over. Maybe a shoulder to cry on was exactly what I needed. Precious had been there for me long enough to see my struggle and my comeback. We had been best friends since elementary school and had been inseparable ever since. She was always there when I needed her and she didn't deserve to be ignored.

BRING FOOD! I texted back to let her know she could come over.

Before she arrived I wanted to get myself together, so I could look somewhat decent. When I looked in the bathroom mirror I didn't recognize who I saw staring back at me. Every emotion I was feeling appeared on my face. The sleepless nights showed in the heavy, dark circles under my eyes. My eyes were red and puffy from the nonstop crying day in and day out. My hair was all over the place and I looked a mess from head to toe. I could visibly see how much skipping meals was taking a toll on my body. My once cute figure was replaced with a frail frame. I was disgusted with what I saw.

"This ain't you Silina, You gotta pull yourself together," I said, giving myself a pep talk as I stared at the woman in the mirror.

I turned on the water in the shower and let the bathroom fill up with steam from the hot water. I peeled my pajamas off and stepped into the shower. The warm water beating down my back felt so good. I squeezed my Dove body wash on my pink pouf and proceeded to scrub like I was trying to wash my sins away.

Suddenly, I felt flutters in my stomach. At first I didn't pay it much attention…until it happened again. Then I realized the funny sensation was my unborn child moving around in my belly. Tears of joy mixed with guilt pooled in my eyes. I couldn't believe that I'd been so wrapped up in my own bullshit that I had put the health of my baby on the back burner. It was that moment that I knew it was time for a change. I was no longer going to feel sorry for myself. I was going to get my life back on track and make the best out of the fucked up situation I was bringing this baby into.

Precious showed up at the door right after I finished getting dressed and doing something to my hair. She came in with bags of Chinese food that smelled so good it caused my mouth to water. I snatched the bags out of her hands and went straight to the kitchen without even saying hello to her.

"Well hello to you too, bitch." She wasted no time getting straight to the point. "You know I'm ready to kick your ass for having me worried like that. I call and text you and get no answer. I come by here and your ass act like you don't see me. What's really going on?" she questioned.

I let out a long, deep sigh. "It's a long story, girl. If it makes you feel any better it wasn't just you that I was ignoring."

"No, actually that doesn't make me feel any better. I don't give a damn who else you're ignoring you should answer the damn phone for *me*. I know that you know I was worried sick.

I could smack you right now! You had my pressure going up and shit behind you. You ain't my man, bitch, so I should not be stressing over you. It's a long story my ass. We got all day. Start talking."

I had gotten us paper plates and filled them up with the shrimp fried rice, general tso chicken, and egg rolls. I was already stuffing my mouth before Precious finished her rant.

"Forgive me, Precious," I said in between chews. "What I'm dealing with right now isn't easy for me to talk about. I'll admit I took the coward's way out and went MIA on everybody. I just needed some time to myself."

"So tell me what's going on. You know damn well you can talk to me about anything. Have I ever judged you before? When you need somebody to lean on that's what you have me for. You don't have to go through anything alone," my friend said, supportively.

"Girl, I walked in on Milan and Chief fucking in my bed."

When those words left my mouth Precious choked on the water she was had just swallowed. I watched the look on her face go from one of concern to complete and total shell shock. She looked like she was trying to figure out if she heard me right.

"What the hell did you just say?" she asked.

"You heard me right. I left Miami early to surprise Chief and came home to find them in my bed." I paused to get myself together. I knew it was going to be hard to talk about, but I didn't think it would be that hard. I was reliving the entire situation all over again.

Precious sat in silence and waited for me to start speaking again. She placed a comforting hand on my shoulder when she saw me getting choked up.

"It's okay. Get it out girl. Don't let that shit build up and put my godchild's health in danger. I can't believe the nerve of those two no account bastards," she said.

"Apparently it wasn't a one–time thing because after I told them to get out of my house, Milan went on to tell me that the secret affair had been going on for two years."

"Oh hell nah! Milan knows she's a dirty bitch for that one. Men will always be men, but that bitch took low to a whole new level. Who would ever think you can't even trust your child around your man? Two years is a long damn time to be creeping. His ass was living a double life. I can't wait to get my hands on Milan, though. She knows Aunt Precious never took any of her bullshit like everybody else did. That's why she can't stand to be around me because she knows I will put her ass in her place. And Chief's ass…you just wait until I see him!" Precious was getting fired up and I could only imagine what she was thinking about doing to them.

Precious didn't play when it came to me. She would never let anybody get away with fucking me over. Even after I handled a situation on my own she would still handle it in her own way. One time I got into a fight in high school and I was beating some girl's ass so all her friends jumped me. Precious

didn't rest until she caught every last one of the bitches one by

one. She waited outside some of their houses, she caught some

of them getting off the school bus, and she fucked one of them

up inside the school bathroom. I knew that she was always

willing to ride with me and I loved her for that.

"You don't have to worry about Chief because he ain't

coming back. I can almost guarantee that you won't be seeing

Milan's scary ass either."

I purposely left out what happened to Chief. Tiana was my

daughter, and I wasn't going to put her freedom at risk by letting

the wrong information get in the wrong hands. I loved Precious

to death and she had never done anything for me to doubt her

loyalty, but I just couldn't bring myself to tell her right then.

"That's some real drama for ya ass girl. Now I completely

understand why you went missing. You needed your time to

heal. I don't want you to dwell on the situation too much longer.

I want you to let go and give it to God. Put yourself and your baby first. You can't change the past, so just take it as a lesson learned and move on. I know it's easier said than done, but time heals all wounds."

"It seems like every time my old wounds heal, new ones replace them. How much can a bitch really take? Besides my brother, all of the other men that have entered my life came in and wreaked havoc." My mind drifted back over twenty years in the past. "For over ten years I was mentally, emotionally, and physically abused by a man, that I believed for the longest time, truly loved me. You know that Shawn was the love of my life. He changed the game up on me as soon as I got pregnant with the twins. The man almost killed me on numerous occasions." Then I decided to confess something to Precious that I had never told her, or anyone else. "The night that Shawn got busted by the Feds was the same night I planned on killing him. I got you to come over and watch the girls so me and Shawn could go to a hotel. I pulled out a gun on him and planned to empty the clip in that motherfucker because I hated him. My plan backfired and he was able to get the gun out of my hands. It was only by the grace of God that the Feds kicked in the door at the exact moment that my life was about to come to an end. God must have known that jail wasn't the route for me to go, so He found another way to get me out of that sticky situation."

Releasing all my demons and getting everything off my chest started to ease my mind a bit. At that moment, I hated myself and everything about my life. I was living in misery for so long that when a glimmer of hope came along I dove in head first, and ended up repeating history all over again. I was broken, confused, and left with a million unanswered questions.

The one thing I did know was that I did not want to become my mother. I was heading down that exact same dreary road that she'd taken. My father had walked out on her, leaving her to take care of two toddlers on her own. He had another family that included a wife and two other kids. My mama stayed by his side for years and then he just up and married another woman, leaving us with nothing.

She started to treat us like she hated us because we were a product of the man that had broken her heart. She went days without feeding us, bathing us, or paying us any attention at all. As young as we were, there was nothing we could do for ourselves. It was a long time ago, but that was a feeling I could never forget. Feeling unwanted and being treated like you were a burden by your own mother was a hard pill to swallow.

After a while I guess she could no longer endure the pain because one night Tony and I went in the bathroom to find our mother sprawled out on the floor with the empty bottle of pills she used to take her own life. We were in the house all week long with her deceased body. We were so young at the time that we thought our mom was sleeping. No matter how much we tried to wake her up, she never did. We didn't know anything about calling 911 or calling anyone for that matter. It wasn't until my grandma came to pick us up for our weekend visit, that my mom's body was discovered. My grandma got all of our belongings and after my mother was buried we never looked back.

"I wanted Shawn's ass dead myself," Precious said snapping me back to the present. "I was so glad when he was finally out of your life because I couldn't stand to see you like that. You weren't yourself at all and you were doing the same thing back then that you're doing now—distancing yourself from everyone. And trying to solve your problems on your own isn't going to help you. All that does is make you more depressed. Everybody needs somebody to lean on. You need to go see a therapist or someone because you have a life that you need to get back to and a business you have to run. One thing that I've learned over the years is that prayer works wonders. You will find peace and understanding when you talk to God no matter what the situation is."

"Look at you getting all religious on me! Since when did you start praying? The only time I've ever known you to get on your knees is when you had a mouthful of dick!"

We both started cracking up at the joke I'd told.

"Laugh all you want, but I'm serious girl. I wake up with a positive mindset every day and I'm at peace with myself. I give all credit to the Most High.

"I know what you mean, P. All bullshit aside. For the past couple of weeks I've been praying so much that my knees hurt. I know He hears my cries and that's why He sent you here. I feel so much better now that I got all off this crap off my chest. The next thing I need to work on is forgiveness because I hate Milan for what she did to me, and that's my own child.

"You can forgive, but that doesn't mean you have to forget. Karma is a bitch and Milan is going to pay for her wrongdoings. It may not be today and it may not be six months from now. But it's definitely going to happen. Now…" she started with a smile on her face. "Go and get dressed, so I can get you out of this house to breathe in some fresh air. And I'm not taking no for an answer. I don't care if I have to drag you out of here kicking and screaming!"

Reluctantly, I got up and went to go throw some clothes on. I didn't feel like getting cute, so I threw on a pair of True Religion jeans with a red V–neck long sleeve shirt. The only reason I agreed to leave the house was because I knew I would never stop hearing Precious' mouth.

"I'ma need for you to get this shit together. You know damn well you ain't supposed to be walking around looking like that. We are about to get you a make–over!" I wasn't insulted by what she'd said because she was right. I couldn't even argue with her. Once we got out the house, I was glad I went. Precious treated me to a day at the spa and I got the works: A full manicure and pedicure, a facial, and a massage. Then afterwards, our next stop was the hair salon.

I walked out of the salon feeling like a brand new woman. I had made a drastic change by getting my hair cut into a short pixie style and having it dyed red. I was loving my new look and couldn't wait to show it off. The whole day was much needed and I couldn't thank Precious enough for helping me in my healing process.

"I guess I can get back to work now just to check on the few things. You mind swinging me by there? I asked Precious.

"Yeah, I got you, boo. Let's go."

"Thank you for being such a good friend, Precious. I love you."

"Don't start getting all mushy on me, girl! You know I love you too. I've got your back no matter what."

It wasn't long before we were walking into my store and it felt good to be back. One of my young employees, Desiree, greeted me as I walked in. "Hey, Ms. Silina. I haven't seen you in a while. I love the haircut! You are looking fierce!"

"Hey, hun! Thank you! I appreciate you helping Precious keep the store running while I was out sick."

"Don't even mention it. You know I'm always willing to help," she said, with her bright smile. She was right too, that's why she was one of my top employees. She made it her business to meet her sales goals every day and then some.

"Before I forget…" Desiree added, "You have a package that came for you this morning."

"Thanks, Desiree. I'll take it in my office and look over it after I review our reports and do some inventory. Again, thanks for all your help," I said, smiling politely as I walked into my office.

Curiosity got the best of me, so I put my work down for a second to see who could have sent me something. The box was unlabeled and it didn't have a return address. I ripped it open. "Aaaagh!" I screamed, jumping back from the box, nearly falling out of my chair. I was shocked to find that someone had wrapped up a dead crow and sent it to me.

Precious busted in my office in a panic. "What's going on in here?"

I looked at the box and she followed my eyes to see exactly what had me so spooked out.

"What the fuck?" was all she could get out.

"You know how I feel about crows. They're a bad omen. This is a sign of bad things to come. Who the fuck would send something like this to me? And why?" I wondered.

CHAPTER 6

Milan

"You let those bitches do this to me! Now I'm going to show you how it feels to get killed while someone you love sits back and watches." I heard a voice say.

The sound of that voice caused the hairs on the back of my neck to stand up. I felt myself shivering and my teeth chattering from fear. I didn't have to see his face to know that it was Chief. I was standing in a long, narrow, dimly lit hallway as I looked around to see where his voice was coming from. I turned around to find that he was standing directly behind me. Shock caused me to jump back and put my hand on my chest to make sure that my heart didn't beat out of it. I was so frightened that it started getting hard for me to control my bladder.

Chief had on all black and the hole in his chest where he'd been shot was still visible. The cut on his face seemed to be getting bigger every second and it was oozing with pus. It looked so disgusting that I had to cover my mouth to keep from throwing up all over him. I tried to take off and run in the opposite direction, but my legs were like lead. They were so heavy it felt like I was trying to run with bricks tied around my ankles.

I looked back to see that Chief was walking closely behind me. He didn't even have to run to keep up with my stride, and the deadly look in his eyes let me know that trouble was brewing. They were like bottomless pits. His eyes were black and cold like a serpent. He had a permanent scowl on his face that made me feel like he was about to snatch my soul right out of my body. I tried with all my might to run as fast as I could and get out of there. The faster I thought I was running, the longer the hallway got. It seemed like it stretched forever, and I started to feel the walls closing in on me.

I felt his hand reach out and grab my shoulder and it was cold and stiff like one of a dead man. I was able to get out of his grasp and start running down the hallway again, but just like before it never ended. I didn't know what to expect, but I did know that I wasn't ready to die. I felt like I was on a trip to hell, and Chief was the devil himself. I was sweating and out of breathe from trying to escape. My hair started to stick to my neck and face which were both drenched with sweat. The next time I looked back was a big mistake because it caused me to trip over absolutely nothing and fall flat on my face.

He grabbed me by my ankle and tried to pull me toward him. My fingernails started peeling back from my skin because I was trying desperately to dig into the ground to avoid his grasp. I was kicking my feet wildly hoping that he would just let me go. I tried to scream for help, but no sound escaped my mouth when I opened it. He came closer and closer. There was nothing I could do. I knew that my time was up and I was going to be living in the pits of hell being tortured for all of eternity. He was like a fire breathing dragon huffing down the back of my neck with his hot breath. I started to gasp for air when I realized that I couldn't breathe. I felt like I was being suffocated, but no one was touching me. The walls started to get tighter and tighter in that never ending hallway, and I started to feel claustrophobic. I watched Chief standing over me laughing an evil, sadistic laugh. My breathing started to slow down until eventually there was no more breath in my body.

I sat straight up in bed, realizing that I just had a horrible nightmare. The images in my mind were so vivid that I couldn't help but wonder what the meaning was.

The smell of fresh cooked bacon filled my nostrils. I sat up and checked out my surroundings and realized that I was still at Elijah's house. He had never mentioned what happened the night he went to find Chief after he'd shot at us. I wasn't sure if he was still lurking or not, and the nightmare I'd had made me fear for my safety. I had been at Elijah's house for almost a month and I always felt safe when he was around. So I wasn't going to allow myself to worry too much. One thing I did know was that I wasn't going back home without a pistol and a few shooting lessons under my belt.

"Good morning, beautiful. I guess I'ma have to throw my pillows in the washing machine 'cause you've slobbered them down," Elijah joked as he came around the corner. "You still got some on the side of your face as a matter of fact," he laughed, as he wiped the side of my face.

I playfully slapped him on his hand, laughing right along with him. "Very funny, nigga!"

"Damn girl, I got your toothbrush and a clean wash cloth in the bathroom waiting for you. You need to go handle that," he said while he was covering his nose with his hand like my breath was funky. I quickly brought my hand to my mouth! I headed toward the bathroom to go handle my business. I knew I had morning breath.

The more I got to know Elijah, the more I realized that he meant what he said about beauty coming from within. I hadn't planned on staying that long, but we were enjoying each other's presence so much, that I didn't want leave. He was such an amazing person to be around. I wanted to stay as long as I could.

The more we got to know each other, the more I started falling for him.

When I started to brush my teeth I felt the sharpest, most intense cramp I'd ever felt in my abdomen. It was like something was trying to tear through my vagina. I doubled over in pain, trying not to make any noise, so I wouldn't alarm Elijah. After a minute or so the pain went away, but it returned two times worse seconds later. I sat down on the toilet, thinking that if I used the bathroom the pain would go away, but when I went to wipe myself, I saw globs of dark bright red blood. I looked inside the toilet and it was filled with blood along with a blood clot the size of a golf ball. The sight of all the blood pouring from my body made me want to pass out.

"What the hell is going on with me?" I wailed.

Suddenly, the pain became too much for me to bear. I fell into a ball on the bathroom floor. I was in the fetal position, praying for God to make all the pain go away. Deep inside I knew exactly what was going on—I was having a miscarriage.

I hadn't had a period in three months, but I was on the move so much that I never gave it any serious thought.

Unbeknown to him or anyone else, I was carrying Chief's child. I didn't know how the fuck I was going to explain that shit to Elijah. I mean what could I say? *I'm in your bathroom losing a baby by the man that tried to kill us not too long ago?* It was no fucking way that I could tell him that. It would completely mess up my plans.

I heard Elijah approaching from down the hall. "You good in there Milan?" he asked, concerned.

"I'm fine," I said in a weak voice. It took everything in me not to scream out in agony.

I guess he could sense the urgency in my voice because he came into the bathroom and found me still balled up on the floor. When he saw all the blood he began to panic.

"What the fuck is wrong with you? Are you okay?" he asked in a panic–stricken tone. He came to my side and lifted me up off the floor, and laid me on his lap.

My voice was so weak. "I–I don't know what's going on," I stuttered. "I really don't know."

"I'm taking you to the hospital. Let's go!" Without waiting for me to protest, he scooped me up and carried me through the house.

He grabbed his keys from the key ring by the front door and we were out. He gently laid me across the back seat of his Camaro, and jumped in the front. He was moving frantically. I had never seen someone so concerned about me. I hadn't known him long, but his actions were already showing me that if I needed him he would be there. He sped out of the parking garage like a bat out of hell, damn near hitting a man who was crossing the street while talking on the phone.

Elijah must've sensed my nervousness because he said, "I'ma get you to the hospital in one piece. You don't have to be scared. I keep telling you to trust me." He flashed that smile that I'd fallen in love with in the rearview mirror. "Talk to me to keep your mind off of the pain." Elijah added.

"Why are you doing all of this for me? I can't remember a time someone looked out for me like you have in the past couple of weeks. To be honest with you, I'm wondering when this nice guy façade will go away and the real Elijah will show up." I knew too well that people made themselves appealing to a person so they could get what they wanted out of them. Once that was accomplished, the script was always flipped. I knew that to be a fact.

"Don't go through life with that mindset because you will fuck around and miss out on something good. I could be your biggest blessing," he answered cockily.

"You're right. You could be. I have really been enjoying your company. I don't think I have ever met anyone as genuine as you. Look, I'm going to need you to let me handle this on my own. I will call you once I find out what's going on. Will you pick me up?" I asked as we pulled up in front of the ER.

"You know I am, girl. I don't even want to leave you here by yourself, but if that's what you want to do, I will respect it.

I got something I need to take care of anyway. Call me as soon as you're ready, and I'll be here," he promised. He exited the car and went into the hospital, bringing a nurse and a wheelchair back out with him.

He watched me until I disappeared behind the doors of the emergency room. In a way, I wished that he could have stayed with me. I hated everything about hospitals, the foul smell, all of the sick ass people every damn where, even the lighting. I didn't like the feeling I got from being in a hospital. It reminded me too much of death. The nurse wheeled me straight to the back and put me in a room.

"Now what seems to be the problem today?" the blonde asked.

I wanted to punch her in her damn face because I didn't know what the fuck she was so jolly about. I guess I was just being a bitch at that moment because I was sulking in misery my damn self.

"Well, as you can see, the problem is I'm bleeding my insides out. So the longer you stand here asking me questions, the more likely it is that I am going to die from blood loss," I said with an attitude, being extra, so that bitch could know she needed to put some pep in her step. I didn't know how much longer I could deal with the pain.

The skinny blonde nurse went and grabbed me a hospital robe, some big ass panties that looked like they were made out of paper, and a pad that was the size of a damn diaper.

"Get undressed and put this on, if you need another sanitary napkin before the doctor comes in, help yourself. The doctor will be in shortly." She exited the room.

Less than five minutes later, the doctor came in the treatment room. After asking me to describe my symptoms, he asked me when my last menstrual cycle was. When I told him that I wasn't sure, the first thing he did was give me an ultrasound to see whether I was pregnant or not. The ultrasound confirmed that I was indeed pregnant, but the fetus in distress.

The doctor told me right away that the baby wasn't going to make it.

I tried to act like I was paying attention to the doctor when he explained to me that I had to have my womb scraped in order to clean out the lining of my uterus. His words had drifted off into thin air because I was lost in my own thoughts.

They couldn't clear my insides out fast enough for me. I didn't want any remnants of Chief's baby to remain inside my body. Now that I knew that I had been pregnant by him when he tried to shoot me made me even angrier than I had been. If Elijah didn't get him the last time, I would make sure he did soon.

When I was finally ready to get discharged, I called Elijah to come pick me up. When he arrived, he was carrying a big brown teddy bear, two dozen red roses, and a balloon that said "Get well soon!" He also had a fresh pair of Levi's jeans and a white Polo v–neck.

"I had to take a lucky guess on the size. I hope they fit," he said, as I sat there speechless. He handed me the clothes first, then walked out the room so that I could dress in private. I couldn't help but smile.

"These jeans are a perfect fit. That was a hell of a lucky guess," I said as I walked out of the room, smiling from ear to ear.

"Well, I might have done a little bit of studying," he grinned, eyeing my curves. I smacked my lips and started giggling.

"You know I can't help but look at you, girl. You've got ass for days. Look at that old man, he's 'bout to break his neck tryna get a glimpse of that booty," he pointed out.

The man looked away embarrassed when he realized he had been caught staring. We both burst out laughing at the look on his face.

"That old man is a perv and so are you," I joked, still laughing with Elijah.

"Can you blame us?" he asked putting this cute, innocent look on his face.

"Hey, thank you for all this. The flowers are beautiful. I love teddy bears too. You didn't have to do all this."

"I love that smile so much that I would do anything to see it on your face," he flirted, wrapping his arm around me and pulling me into a warm embrace.

As we walked to the car, he broke his embrace and stepped a few paces ahead of me so that he could open my door. It seemed like every second I was around him he showed me more of himself, and I liked what I was seeing. I had never come across a man as charming as him before. This made me wonder how old he was, because apparently, I had looking in the wrong age bracket before. Chivalry was definitely dead in the late 80's and 90's generation.

"Thank you," I said politely, when he got in the car with me.

"You don't have to keep thanking me for doing things that a man is supposed to do for a woman." He smiled.

"How old are you, if you don't mind me asking?"

"I will be 28 in four months," he responded. "May to be exact. What made you ask that?"

"I was just curious. That's all. I thought you were older because of all of the wisdom and good manners you have. I thought chivalry was dead in this fucked up generation, but I guess not. It seems like your mama raised you right." I complimented.

"Sounds like you just been fucking with the wrong niggas," he countered.

"Tell me about it," I muttered in a barely audible tone. "You have accomplished a lot to be so young. That's something that's rare these days. I'm trying to have something established by the time I'm your age—within the next four years."

"You can do it too. All you have to do is set small goals and do everything necessary to achieve them. Once you knock those out, it will become easier for you to achieve the bigger goals. It's nothing that you can't do if you put in the work," he assured me. "I've been out here grinding for my own since I was 14. All I do is progress and I plan to keep on progressing. I will never get content and that's why I've already accomplished a lot. So is everything okay with you? What exactly happened at the emergency room?"

I hung my head down in shame and avoided eye contact with him as I spoke. "I–I had a miscarriage," I whispered.

"You had *what*?" he asked with a puzzled expression. He was looking at me like I had grown another head.

"Please listen to my story before you judge me." I let out a deep breath. "The pregnancy was the result of a rape. I never told anyone about this, so please don't make it any harder than it already is for me. I looked out of the corner of my eye to see if he was falling for my award–winning performance.

"I'm here for you, Milan. I never judge anyone. If you want to talk about it, I'm willing to listen."

I let out another sigh and forced some tears to roll down my cheeks. "Chief was the one who raped me. One day I told him that I was no longer going to be his personal drug mule, and he got real violent with me. He had his way with me and left me laying there like I was a piece of trash. I felt so dirty, so disgusting, and so humiliated. I didn't think that anyone would believe me if I told them. I just found out I was pregnant and lost a baby all in the same day. And it was all because of a man who raped and tried to kill me." On cue I burst out in tears.

Elijah rubbed my back soothingly. I could tell that he was at a loss for words, but he was still trying to comfort me.

"You did find him that night...didn't you?" I asked in between fake sobs.

"I searched for him high and low and I had some of my people looking for him too. But it was like he just fell off the face of the earth. Nobody has seen or heard from him in a while from my understanding. Everybody said he went missing and been MIA ever since. I still have people looking for him and I put the word out that I have $100,000 for anyone that can bring him to me alive. I'm going to make sure that he pays for what he did to you. I won't stop until he takes his last breath." The anger written on his face let me know that he meant exactly what he'd said.

"Make sure that I'm around to witness it. I want to be the one that ends his miserable life."

"Does your family know anything about this?" he questioned.

"I don't have any family, I'm on my own. All I have is me. Family will hurt you worse than a person on the streets will."

"Don't worry about it, ma. Chief's gonna get got. It ain't enough room for the both of us in these streets, so he has to go!"

Mission accomplished. Chief, your life is on a countdown!

We went back to Elijah's place. When I walked in the dining room table was set for two. He had it set up with champagne chilling on a bucket of ice, two crystal flutes, and a bouquet of fresh assorted flowers as the centerpiece. The flames from burning candles were flickering and R. Kelly's new CD was playing in the background. He had all the components of a romantic evening spread out in front of me and I hadn't even expected it. It felt good to have somebody that wanted to give me all the things a woman deserved.

"I don't know what to say," I whispered.

"Well don't say anything. Come sit with me and enjoy this meal."

He proceeded to pull out my chair, so I could have a seat at the table. He went to the kitchen for a few minutes and came back with two plates of crab legs, buffalo shrimp, baked potatoes, and broccoli. I was hoping that the meal tasted as good as it appeared because I was starving. I didn't waste any time diving in and indulging in the delicious spread.

"Damn girl, I've never seen a female clean off a plate like that," Elijah joked. He had a sense of humor that I loved.

"You're damn right! I'm not about to let none of this good food go to waste. I love me some seafood too I'm a fat kid at heart," I laughed, cracking myself up while sticking my tongue out at him for sending shots at me.

"I see. All that weight your ass is toting had to come from somewhere," he replied with a smile.

I had to admit that I was starting to like the young man. He was such a gentleman and he had everything a woman could ever dream of. He did the little things that every woman wished their man would do for them. The way he made me feel was a new experience for me, but I liked it.

After we ate he started rolling up a Backwood. The way he was rolling that blunt with his lips and tongue had me wondering what else that mouth could do. I couldn't tell what he was saying, but he was mumbling something to himself. He looked like he was in deep thought, and I could tell something was bothering him.

"What's the matter with you?" I asked.

"I can't sleep until that nigga is dead. I'm too paranoid to be playing with my life like that. This is one of those situations

I was telling you about before. I have to get him before he gets me. And I'll be damn if I let anything happen to you. I'm going to ride home with you tomorrow and fly back out here and handle my business. I don't want to get you caught in the middle of no bullshit, so I think it's best if you go back to Virginia. If he is after me then he won't bother you, but just in case, I have something for you." He put the perfectly rolled blunt down on the table and went to the hallway closet. He came back with a small black handgun. "Keep this with you at all times and make sure you always play it safe. You need to move out of your mother's house so that he won't know where to find you. I'll give you the money to get you a new crib."

"I don't stay with my mama anymore. I told you I don't have family. I'm on my own and I'm struggling to pay these bills which was why I came down to Maryland in the first place...remember?"

"Well I know you're glad that I made you quit while you were ahead. Don't worry about the money. I got you. I'll send you back with something and you can call me if you ever need anything."

"I'm going to miss you," I pouted.

"You'll see me again soon. Don't worry about that." He picked up the blunt, lit it and inhaled deeply. After a few puffs he passed it to me.

I didn't usually smoke because I hated the way that shit made my hair smell, but I decided to go ahead and enjoy my last night with Elijah.

"Damn girl, pass that. You over there cheifin' and shit," Elijah joked.

By the time I realized it, I had damn near faced the whole L. The shit hit me all at once and I started tripping. I didn't know what the fuck we were smoking on, but it damn sure was some potent shit. My body was still there with Elijah, but my mind had drifted off to the clouds. I felt like I was floating on air. I was in this peaceful, tranquil like state. I saw that Elijah's lips were moving, but I didn't hear anything he was saying. The only thing that I heard was silence. It was like trying to hear while being submerged in water. It was impossible for me to hear anything going on around me. I felt myself drifting further and further away from reality.

The next thing I knew, I went from being at peace to feeling like I was paralyzed. I was aware of my surroundings and I could clearly see what was going on around me, but I couldn't move one inch of my body. It was as if someone was holding me down with all their might and I was fighting a losing battle to get up. I tried so hard to open my mouth and speak, but no sound ever escaped my lips. I was having an out of body experience. It was like I was hovering over myself watching everything take place, but there was nothing that I could do or say. I watched Elijah ask me if I was going to be okay, but I couldn't respond. That was the last thing I remembered before I slipped into the darkness that awaited me.

CHAPTER 7

Silina

"Alright, Mrs. Smith, it looks like you've got a healthy baby boy in there! Congratulations, hun," my doctor announced cheerfully, while wiping away the cold gel used for ultrasounds.

"Thank you, doctor. I'm so excited. After all these years, I'll finally get to see what it's like to raise a little man," I gushed.

"I'm glad you finally got your wish. I know your husband is going to be thrilled when he finds out. Before you leave stop at the front desk and schedule an appointment for same time next month. Have a good day and take care of yourself and that little one," she said with a warm smile.

I loved Dr. Weiss. She had been my doctor since I delivered the twins 23 years ago. I couldn't believe that I was finally having the little boy I'd always wanted. It was a bitter sweet moment for me because Chief had always talked about wanting a little boy and he wouldn't even be around to see it. Just hearing the doctor mention him made me cringe. I didn't know if I would be able to deal with seeing his face without wanting to hurt him all over again. Even though a couple of months had passed, the pain in my heart still had not eased up yet. I wasn't even sure if I had a heart anymore because it felt more like a void that would never be filled.

There wasn't a day that had passed that I didn't wonder what had happened to Chief that night. Tony was keeping his eyes and ears to the streets, but no one had seen or heard from Chief or so I'd been told. I still couldn't believe that he had just disappeared like that. Many nights I woke up in a cold sweat from having nightmares. I felt like I was on the run. I was constantly looking over my shoulder. I was paranoid as hell because I didn't know if Chief was watching and waiting, but I had a feeling that he was. No one ever said anything about finding his body, so I knew deep down that he was still alive. I knew him like the back of my hand. He was probably waiting for the perfect moment to get his payback. I knew that he wouldn't do anything to harm me while I was carrying his child. I was more afraid for my daughters' lives than anything.

I wasn't going to let anything steal my joy at that moment, though because I was elated to find out that I was having a baby boy. My girls and I had been praying for a boy to love on and spoil. Well, maybe we wouldn't spoil him *that* much because I couldn't deal with another spoiled child.

As soon as I walked out of the doctor's office, my cell phone started ringing. I pulled it out and saw that it was my daughter, London, calling.

"Hey, Lon, guess what? We're having a boy!" I chimed into the phone before she could even say hello.

"Mama, how long will it be before you get home?" London said in a shaky voice. The tone in her voice alarmed me because she was usually the calm, cool, and collected one.

"I'm on my way home now. What's going on, London?" I asked, trying to remain calm.

"Just get home as fast as you can," she said, with panic in her voice. "I don't think I should say anything over the phone," she stated cryptically.

"Girl, you know my damn nerves are bad and you're calling my fucking phone with something that sounds like an emergency, but you won't tell me what it is? You better stop fucking with me and talk, little girl! As a matter of fact, never mind. I'll be there in less than ten minutes!" I yelled.

I pulled up to my house and had barely put the car in park before I was waddling up the driveway. My protruding baby bump was slowing me down, so I knew I wasn't moving as fast as I felt like I was. When I looked up at my house, I noticed that two of the windows in the front of my house had been busted out. My heart started racing and a huge lump formed in my throat. A million different scenarios played out in my head within seconds, and I didn't like any of them. I turned around and went back to my car to grab the .22 I kept in my glove compartment for protection.

I was nervous as hell as I approached the house because I didn't know what to expect, but I knew I had to shake that shit off and go make sure that my daughters were safe. I walked into the house and was horrified to see that everything had been completely trashed. The curtains had been snatched down from the broken windows, the couches were ripped apart and overturned, and the TV was face down on the floor. The mirrors that had once hung in my living room were shattered. It looked like a tornado had ripped through my house. My heart was beating like a bass drum as I moved frantically around the house to find my girls.

"London! Tiana!" I yelled through the house, running from room to room.

A few seconds later, London came running out of her room with a disturbed look on her face.

"Is everything okay, baby? Are you hurt?" I asked, scanning her face and body to make sure that she wasn't harmed. "You weren't in the house when this happened, were you?"

"I'm fine, Ma. I came home from school and I noticed that the front windows were busted. The first thing I thought was somebody tried to rob us. So I came in the house to see what was missing, but I saw that everything was still here. It was just trashed. I walked through the entire house to make sure nobody was here and when I went in the kitchen I found this taped to the refrigerator." She handed me a crumbled up piece up paper.

You better watch your back. I'm gonna get you!! Your past will come back to haunt you. You are going to die, Silina.

After reading the note one time, the contents of my stomach made its way back up my esophagus and onto the floor. I accidentally threw up all over London's shoes and the disgust showed on her face. She discarded the shoes and socks in the kitchen and came back with a glass of ice cold water for me. My palms were sweating and my whole body was shaking like a leaf on a tree. The moment that I was dreading had finally come. I looked at the paper again and realized that the words had been written in blood. I tried to make out the handwriting but it didn't look familiar.

"We need to call Uncle Tony and let him handle this. I'm sure that somebody done ran their mouth by now and somebody is talking about who broke in Silina and Chief's house." London said.

London put her arm around me and walked me through the catastrophe that I once called a living room. She motioned for me to sit down on one of the bar stools in the kitchen. She then got a cool wash cloth and started to dab my forehead with it. I didn't know what I would do without my daughter. If it wasn't for her, I probably would have been admitted into the psych ward with everything that was going on. She had really been there for me, and I couldn't express my gratitude enough.

"Did you see anything suspicious when you were pulling up to the house?" I questioned, my voice trembling. I was scared shitless, but I tried to hide it so my daughter wouldn't start panicking. It seemed like she was the one trying to remain calm for the both of us.

"Now that you mention it, I did see a black Lincoln that I had never seen out here before. When I was turning on our street, they were leaving, headed in the opposite direction. I didn't catch any faces because of the dark tint, but they were speeding like they were trying to get the hell out of Dodge," she recalled.

"Fuck! This shit's gotta be the work of Chief or some of his people. I knew that his ass was coming sooner or later. I should have prepared for this day because I swear I saw the shit coming," I admitted. "First the dead crow sent to my store and now this. It has to be the Chief fucking around with me."

"Or it could be Milan's salty ass trying to scare you. She's probably still feeling some type of way about getting disowned. I haven't seen or heard anything about her ass. Tiana has been trying to reach out to her, but she hasn't heard a single word from her either. I doubt that Chief would try to kill you while you're carrying his baby," London tried to reason.

She did have a point, but I couldn't be too sure. I couldn't cancel anyone out knowing that my life was probably on a countdown. London was right. Maybe Milan was doing this shit to us just to scare us. I knew that if it was her, there was no way in hell that she would kill me for real. I honestly didn't know whose work this was, but I knew I wasn't going to get caught slipping. If someone did try to take me out, they were going to have a hell of a fight on their hands.

"We can sit here and try to figure out who's behind this but the truth is we don't know for sure. My name was on the note, so y'all are probably safe. It's *me* that they're after, but I want you and Tiana to keep y'all eyes and ears open. They might try to use one of y'all to get to me, so stay on your P's and Q's. Where the hell is Tiana anyway?" I panicked.

"She was with her boo last time I talked to her, but when I told her what had happened, she said she was on her way. She

123

should be here soon. And Ma, you know we got your back. You are not alone in this. If I have to stay by your side and not let you out of my sight, then that's what I'll do. Think about it, though. If someone really wanted to kill you and they know where we live already, then why wouldn't they just do that instead of trashing all our stuff? This seems like the work of a jealous, hating ass broad and not of a cold blooded killer," she pointed out.

"I'm not about to take any chances with my life or any of my kids. I'm going to file a police report, so they can have everything on the record. I'm also about to get the locks changed and get security bars added to every window in the house. Security cameras will be installed. I want to see every movement that goes on in and around my house. We can't be too careful. Don't forget that we don't know if Chief is dead or not. If he isn't, there's no telling what's going to happen to me."

I only prayed that God was on my side because right then, I needed Him more than ever.

CHAPTER 8

Tiana

There was loud banging at the door that snatched me from my sleep. "Open up! It's the police!"

I wiped the crust from my eyes and threw on my robe to go see what all the commotion was about. Before I got a chance to open the door it was being kicked off the hinges, almost taking me down to the floor with it. Immediately the house was swarming with federal agents and detectives.

"Why the fuck is y'all up in my house and what are you looking for? I hope you have a warrant to be all up in my shit, breaking doors down and what not," I shouted at all of them over the mayhem they were causing..

One of them sons of bitches grabbed me by my arm and tried to manhandle me. I wasn't having that shit, so I went off. I started throwing hands and the old ass white man that was putting his crusty ass hands on me didn't stand a chance. The next thing I knew I was being thrown on the floor by damn near the whole police force. It took a few of them motherfuckers to take me down because I wasn't going out without a fight. I still didn't know what was going on and what they were doing in my house. So as far as I was concerned, they were the ones violating me and my territory.

"Tiana Gellar, you are under arrest for the attempted murder of Clayton Smith. You have the right to remain silent. Anything you say can and will be used against you in a court of law…."

The rest of the words disappeared into thin air because my mind went completely blank. I didn't say a word because I didn't want to incriminate myself any further. I had a feeling that this day would come and I was ready for it. I felt the cold metal being secured around my wrists and cutting into my flesh. I instinctively tried to wriggle my wrists, but the cuffs were so tight that I felt like if I made one false move, I would injure myself.

"Who the fuck told on me? If I find out that anybody snitched on me, they will regret it."

I was confident to know that these bastards damn sure weren't gonna find any physical evidence that could tie me to any attempted murder. But it was going to be a different story if they had a witness' testimony. I felt my chest beginning to tighten up as I took the walk of shame. Neighbors had come outside to stand on their porches to see what all the raucous was about in the normally quiet community. I was escorted to the police car and carelessly thrown into the back seat like I was a fucking zoo animal. I looked them motherfuckers dead in their eyes with the meanest scowl on my face to let them know that I wasn't scared. And I gave them a smirk to tell them "Let the games begin". The door slammed in my face and the sirens blared as we sped off to the precinct.

I jumped up out of my sleep and looked around to find that I was still in my bed in my room. I had been having that same nightmare every night for the past few months. I couldn't tell whether it was a sign or if it was just my guilty conscience fucking with me. I felt in my heart that the day would come when either the police or the streets were definitely coming for me. Until then, I was going to continue living my life like there was no tomorrow. I wasn't about to live in fear for nobody. I was woman enough to handle any consequences that I'd brought upon myself. I didn't even mean to shoot Chief, but when I saw him coming toward me I felt the need to protect myself.

I had spent half of my life watching my mother get her ass beat every single day. I experienced firsthand what it did to her mentally, physically, *and* emotionally. I'd heard the lies she told to people when they would ask her about her latest black eye, bloody nose, or bruised ribs. I had witnessed the pain she experienced when she was isolated from her family, friends, and her job. I'd seen the fear in her eyes each time she saw my father enter a room. My mother had completely lost herself behind a man who had rather beat her unconscious than love her. My dad knew that my mom was too good for him, so he'd made her feel like she was less of a woman when it was really him that was a worthless man.

My dad was nothing but an abusive alcoholic in my eyes. He was a good provider, but he would come home drunk and start fights with my mother for no apparent reason. At first, she used to fight him back, but after a while, it was like she lost every bit of fight in her. Just watching him make my mom cry, made me want to kill him, even as young as I was. I couldn't even have a real father slash daughter bond with him because of how he treated her. I couldn't lie and say that he was a bad father because he treated his girls like princesses. He spent time with us, we did things together on the weekends, and he spoiled us with gifts. From the outside looking in, you would've thought we were all a big happy family.

After ten long years of agony, the Feds kicked the door in on him and my mom and got him on kingpin charges. There were rumors going around that my mom had snitched on him, but I never found that to be true. I knew that she was too afraid of him to ever tell on him. Fear was what kept her living in hell for over ten years. I was not the least bit sad when the judge ruled and gave him 25 years to life. As a matter of fact, that was the day that life began for me.

I was ecstatic to see that my mama had finally gotten her *oomph* back after being so damaged. She didn't let that situation break her and take control of her life. She used it as a learning experience, and it made her a stronger woman. I wasn't too happy when she introduced us to Chief because I thought that she was moving too fast by jumping into another relationship. Plus there was something about Chief that I just didn't like. He was a nice man and he treated my mom wonderfully, but he seemed like a big ass fraud to me. I decided to let it go and be cordial toward him for my mama's sake because it was her life. And for the first time, she seemed genuinely happy.

The truth is, when I shot Chief all I saw was flashes of my childhood. I had witnessed my mama getting smacked around one too many times. So Chief just happened to be the one to catch my wrath. When I shot him, I saw my father's face. I didn't think twice about it and I didn't even flinch when I pulled the trigger. I knew my mama was probably thinking I was a cold–blooded murderer by the way I had handled that glock. She never asked me about it because we promised to never discuss what had happened that night again. But I knew that all types of questions were floating through her mind. I had never shot anyone before, but I wouldn't hesitate to do it again if it came down to protecting my family. My mama and my sisters were all I had.

"Damn, I got some real Lifetime movie bullshit going on in my life right now," I said to myself as I sat up in my bed.

I was still trying to figure out who was behind the break in at our house. Nothing made sense at that point. I didn't know which way to point the finger because I figured that it would have been me that Chief wanted dead, but the note that was left in the house specifically mentioned my mom. She didn't know it, but I had some of my male friends watching her every move. There was no way I was going to lose her. So if me or London couldn't be with her, we made sure we kept eyes on her at all times.

"All this bullshit is going on because Milan wanted to share some dick with her own damn mama. I could choke that bitch out right now. People's lives are on the line now!" I vented aloud.

Just then London announced, "That's why when I see that bitch, it's gonna be World War III out this bitch. I can't wait to cross her path because I am going to make her life a living hell."

"Closed doors mean do not enter unless you knock, bitch!" I said, rolling my eyes. I smacked my teeth, so she would know that I didn't appreciate her invading my privacy.

"Girl boo!" she gave me the talk to the hand gesture and came and plopped her funky ass on my bed. "You know there ain't no such thing as privacy when you're living up in your mama's house. You don't pay no bills in this bitch, heifer."

We looked at each other and burst out in a fit of giggles. We could always count one another to lift each other's spirits.

"I still think that Milan is behind this whole ordeal. She probably just wanted to get back at Mama and try to scare us. Why don't we go talk to her ourselves and find out what the fuck is really up? If she don't wanna give up any answers, then I will gladly beat them out of her. Maybe her and Chief are plotting on us together. We still don't know for a fact that he is dead. If he isn't, there is a pretty good chance that he and Milan are plotting revenge. Let's get them before they get us." An evil smirk spread across London's face.

"I wish I could say that Milan wouldn't do something like that, but she showed me that I can't put anything past her ass. You could be right about her, but how would we even be able to find her? I haven't heard from her since she left the house. If she did have something to do with it or even knew about it, why would she tell us?" I wondered.

"Luckily for us I have friends in high places. My college friend is a realtor, and she told me that she rented out a condo to my twin sister. I was able to get her to tell me that Milan gave up $14,000 cash to pay her rent upfront for a year. She also said that she had a male friend that comes by there on a regular basis. That mysterious male friend could be Chief." London had a satisfied look on her face like she had just solved the mystery of the century.

"Okay, Nancy Drew, since you have it all figured out, I will follow your lead. If the mystery man is Chief, and we find out that he and Milan responsible for all the turmoil, I promise this time I won't miss with the kill shot."

The idea of Milan working with Chief to plot against her own damn family made my blood boil. I loved my sister, but I damn sure wasn't about to let her take us down behind a dumb ass decision that she had made. Nobody was going to threaten my mama's life.

"Well let's find out, gangster. I have the address. Get dressed and meet me at the car in twenty minutes. Don't mention any of this to Mama because I haven't told her anything I know yet. She doesn't need to be stressing while she's carrying our baby brother. She already has enough on her plate."

"You think I don't know that, bitch? Go get dressed, so we can find out what the fuck is really going on," I ordered.

I didn't waste any time getting ready to go play Inspector Gadget. I wanted to get to the bottom of things and make our little problem go away, so we could live our lives in peace. After taking a shower, brushing my teeth, and throwing on some black sweat pants and a Nike t–shirt with some sneakers, we were out. London had already beat me to the car, and was waiting impatiently.

"It took your ass long enough! I thought I was gonna have to come drag you out of the house."

"I would have been the last bitch you ever dragged too," I retorted.

She sped out of the driveway and headed toward the I–264.

We ended up in downtown Norfolk. We stopped in front of a high rise building on Granby Street. It looked like a luxury apartment building. I was curious to know how Milan was able to afford some fancy shit like this.

"So what do we do now, private investigator?" I asked London.

"We wait and we watch. I want to see if we can catch anything suspicious before we go Rambo on her ass."

We sat in the car for half an hour before we saw anything that caught our eye. I kept seeing police ride by and getting nervous as hell. I hated the fucking police, and prayed that I never had to ride in the back of one of those cars.

When I looked up, I saw Milan walking out of the building. She was dressed in a black bustier, black booty shorts, fishnet stockings and some thigh high black boots with six inch heels.

Her jet black hair was styled in spiral curls. She looked like she was about to go work on somebody's fucking corner. She had a man on her arm, but it damn sure wasn't Chief. It was a fine ass dark skin man that I had never seen before. They were laughing and giggling as they walked down the street. I watched the man open the passenger door of a navy blue Camaro and help Milan inside.

"There goes our mystery man, but that damn sure don't look like Chief or any one of his goons," London announced.

"Looks like Milan done found herself a new man," I replied.

I suddenly felt ridiculous stalking my sister like she was some fucking prey. I will admit that what London had said did make a lot of sense at first. But what I had just seen with my own eyes was confusing to me. We watched the blue car pull off and before I could even say a word, London started following them. We didn't follow them for long before the car pulled up in front of Paradise. It was a bar that had just recently opened on Granby Street and was getting a lot of buzz.

We watched the man get out and walk around to open the door for Milan to exit the car. The two shared a passionate kiss and he grabbed a handful of her voluptuous ass before she disappeared into the bar. It was obvious that Milan didn't pay attention to her surroundings because if she did she would have definitely seen us.

"So what now, genius? It doesn't look like Milan is plotting any revenge to me. It just looks like she found her a new man who obviously cares about her enough to take care of her. Maybe he paid for her new condo. I don't see Chief anywhere in the mix," I stated. I was irritated by then because I felt like I had just wasted a lot of my precious time on a dummy mission.

"It still wouldn't hurt to ask questions and find out what's really going on. If she is behind this, do you really think that she would be stupid enough to be seen with Chief? Milan knows we're smarter than that, so she's going to always try to be one step ahead of us," London pointed out.

"Well it looks like we're at a dead end right now, 'cause it ain't no way in hell I'm going into that bar looking like this."

"Well I'm going in, so I guess your ass is just gonna have to wait in the car. Shit! Who the hell are you tryna impress any damn way?"

"*Nobody*. It's just the principle."

London waved me off and rolled her eyes. It was a good thing that it was Happy Hour, so you didn't have to be all fancy. London didn't look half bad, though. She had on black Victoria's Secret Pink joggers and a matching v neck t–shirt. It wasn't her normal dolled up look, but we had come here for a purpose, so she didn't give a damn. I watched her strut her ass up to the door and enter the bar. I prayed for Milan's sake that this was all a big misunderstanding. If things didn't go in London's favor, I knew that shit would get real bad, real fast.

CHAPTER 9

Milan

"Well, well, well, look who we have here." I heard a familiar voice say over my shoulder. I turned around to be greeted by my twin sister, London.

"Bitch, what the fuck are you doing here?" I spat. I was really wondering how the hell she had found me. I was ready to fuck her up on sight because of how dirty she had treated me the last time I saw her.

I checked out my surroundings to make sure I wasn't about to be under attack. London would be on some dumb shit like that. I didn't even know why the hell she was so hung up on the situation. It wasn't like I had fucked *her* man.

"Having flashbacks of the last time I beat that ass, huh?" she taunted.

I wanted to smack that smirk right off of her face, but going to jail for getting into a bar fight with my twin was not an option.

"What the fuck do you want? I'm trying to enjoy my drink and I'm expecting somebody. " I snapped. A few people looked over at us to see what was going on, and I just smiled politely at them.

"Oh, you mean that sexy chocolate thang you were with earlier? Yeah, he is fine girl! Kudos to you, though. You look like you're doing pretty well for yourself. That's a nice condo you're living in, girl. You should invite me over some time. Hey, how about you get me a drink? I'll take a shot of peach Ciroc on the rocks." She winked at me and clapped her hands like I was her personal servant.

She was definitely about to make me lose my entire cool. I closed eyes and said a silent prayer. *Jesus keep me near the cross.*

"Are you fucking stalking me, bitch? Get a life and move on because I have. I'm not thinking about any of y'all!"

"I just came here to see what's going on with you and Chief," she blurted out. "I know that you and him had something to do with fucking up our crib."

My ears perked up at the mention of Chief's name. From what I had heard, it was obvious that he wasn't just after me. That bastard was out to get *everybody*. They must have thought that I had something to do with it, not knowing that Chief was after me too.

"I don't know what the fuck you're talking about. I have shit to do, so can you get the fuck out of my face and stay out of my life?"

"If I find out that you had any part in this, I am gonna personally make you pay. You know it will bring me so much pleasure to torture you. You will be able to scream as loud as you want, but nobody will hear you." She put her arm around me and pulled me in closer. "You can take me for a joke if you want to," she whispered. "But you know me. I make good on my threats, and you know it baby. Love ya, sis!" she chuckled, before pushing past me as she exited the bar.

I walked out of the bar behind her to go see if Elijah had found somewhere to park yet. Lost in my thoughts and paying no mind to where I was walking, I wound up walking down an empty one–way street instead of going down the street the parking garage was on. It was easy to get these those streets downtown confused when it was dark. It was too damn dark for my liking, and there weren't enough people around for me. I kept looking back because I felt like somebody was following me.

I pulled out my phone to call Elijah and tell him that I had walked down the wrong street and I was on my way back. An eerie feeling went through my entire body as I dialed his number. I tried to brush it off and I put some pep in my step. The spring breeze was whipping my hair all over the place, and suddenly a man that was jogging with a black hoodie on bumped into me and made me drop my phone straight to the concrete.

"Excuse you, motherfucker!" I shouted to the unknown man "I know you saw me right here!" He never stopped jogging or looked back.

I bent down to pick up my phone and discovered that it was completely shattered. I tried to cut it back on, but the screen went completely black. I started walking a little bit faster once I realized that I was out here with no means of communication. Walking down that long dark road made the walk seem even more dreadful. I got nervous as hell.

I noticed a dark colored truck creeping down the road. I wouldn't have thought anything of it if the driver wasn't going so far below the speed limit. The closer the car got to me, the slower it went. My heart was pounding and I was damn near running to try to get away. I couldn't walk fast enough to get away from the car that was now creeping to a stop right beside me.

"Bring that ass here, girl," I heard a voice say.

The voice caused me just stand there, frozen in fear. I couldn't move. Hell, I could barely breathe. I didn't even have to look up to see whose voice it was. Once I looked back and realized that my worst fear had come true, I tried to take off running. I didn't get too far before I was swept off my feet and thrown into the back of the truck.

I looked up and saw the nasty scar on the right side of his face.

Please don't let him kill me in this truck, God. If you're listening, please save me.

"Damn, Milan, that's how you do? I put you on and gave you a way to make a lot of money, and you pay me back by fucking my plug? That's some low shit!"

"Did you forget that you are married to my mama and you were cheating on her with me? What's some low shit is you shooting to try to kill me! What the fuck did I ever do to you?"

"You were disloyal to me. You happened to be at the wrong place at the wrong time. When I noticed it was you with E when I tried to take him out, I realized what was going on. So I didn't give a fuck about taking you out right along with him."

"Why are you trying to take him out after all this time? I just don't get it."

"It's not for you to get, sweet thang," Chief started rubbing on my thighs. This time it didn't turn me on. It grossed me out. The only person I wanted touching me was Elijah, and I hoped that he would come to my rescue.

Chief came closer to me in the back seat and tried to kiss me. I took the heel of my boot and shoved it in his stomach area before he even knew what had hit him. That caused him to double over in pain and I used that opportunity to pull out the small gun that I had tucked in my boot. I aimed it directly at Chief's head.

He started laughing when he saw me aiming the gun at him. "What are you going to do...shoot me too?"

I cocked my gun back to let him know that I wasn't playing any game. The only thing I that kept replaying in my head was Elijah saying "kill or be killed." I knew that this was one of those situations that he was talking about.

"Not so fast, bitch!"

I felt cold steel on the back of my head. I had my gun aimed at Chief, and the passenger of the truck had one to my dome.

Damn, I done fucked up now!

CHAPTER 10

London

Something wasn't sitting right with the whole ordeal my mother was going through. Tiana wanted me to leave it alone because she started to doubt that Milan had anything to do with it. I thought otherwise based on the way she had acted when I caught her at the bar. When I mentioned Chief's name, her eyes got wide like her secret had been exposed. She was probably shocked that I was on to her ass. I decided to do a little bit more investigating because I couldn't cancel anybody out with my mother's life on the line.

I decided to pay her another visit after I dropped Tiana off at home that night. I wasn't just about to take her word for it because her word held no weight with me. I popped up at her house and knocked on her door. When she didn't come to the door, I knocked again. She was probably looking out the peep hole, watching me knock.

Out of nowhere the man that we saw Milan with the day before came into the hallway.

"Damn, Milan, you had me worried about you. I've been calling you and getting your voicemail. Everything good with you?" he asked.

Since Milan and I were identical twins, and I had a long weave, I could easily be mistaken for her. It was obvious that he thought I was Milan, especially since I was standing outside her door. I realized that this was the perfect chance to make Milan feel the same pain that she had made our mom endure.

"Yeah, I'm good. I tried to call you before you came inside the bar to tell you that I wasn't feeling it and I wanted to go home but my phone went dead. I came home to change and charge my phone up. I was just about to run to the store and my dumb ass locked my keys in the house. I forgot that I changed purses and left my keys in the other bag. I'm sorry I didn't mean to have you worried," I responded, going along.

"That's some sappy shit to do girl. You could have just waited at the bar until I came in and told me that you wanted to leave. It's too much shit going on for you to just up and leave like that without letting me know something. Here, I have the spare key on me."

He unlocked the door and let me enter the house first. When I stepped inside I was impressed by how Milan was living. She had a cute little red living room set that she had accentuated with zebra print pillows. The curtains that covered her balcony door were sheer black, and she had red vertical blinds. Her large flat screen TV was mounted on the wall.

"Why don't you put those pots and pans to use and cook me a meal," he said.

"I can do that for you, boo," I flirted.

I walked into the kitchen and went through her refrigerator and cabinets to see what she was working with. It damn sure wasn't much because Milan's ass had never cooked a meal a day in her life. I found a bag of chicken wings and some rice.

There was a bag of broccoli in the freezer, so I decided to do something with that. I whipped up some chicken, rice, and homemade gravy with broccoli on the side.

"It's about time I got a home cooked meal from you," he said, devouring every morsel of the meal I had placed in front of him.

"Don't worry, there's plenty more where that came from," I flirted.

"I like the sound of that. For a minute I was afraid that you couldn't even cook," he laughed.

"There isn't too much that I can't do."

I saw why Milan had fallen for the man. He was fine as hell, and I knew she had radar for niggas with money. His whole persona screamed that he was about that cash, and I knew that she was willing to hop on the first thing she could when she got kicked out on her ass.

He seductively licked his lips and gave me a sexy smirk. He had those soft, luscious lips that made you want to kiss them. I was ready to see how much fun I could have with him.

"You tryna take a couple of shots with me?" I asked, pulling out the bottle of Hennessy I'd spotted on Milan's counter.

"That depends. Are you trying to get me drunk, so you can have your way with me?"

"Why don't you stop asking questions and find out what I'm trying to do," I replied seductively.

He took the Henny out of my hand and took a big gulp straight from the bottle. He passed the bottle back to me, and I took it to the head. He stood behind my spot on the couch and started to massage my shoulders.

"Mmm, that feels good." His hands were like magic, working my shoulders.

"Lay down on your stomach for me."

"What do you have up your sleeve?

"Just do what I asked you and trust me."

I wasted no time laying down to see what he had in store for me. When I lay down, I felt his strong, masculine hands creeping up my back. He had lifted my shirt up and pulled it over my head in one swift motion. He unsnapped my bra and removed that too. His hands were massaging my back. He replaced his hands with his lips, placing soft kisses down my spine. It felt euphoric. I sat up and faced him then stared deeply into his eyes before sharing one of the most passionate kisses ever.

I completely understood what people meant when they said that they saw fireworks from their first kiss. I had never seen fireworks before, but the sparks were damn sure flying right then. Soon we couldn't keep our hands off of each other.

He picked me up and walked down the hallway to Milan's bedroom. I was hoping that she wouldn't come home and interrupt what I had going on with her man because I was ready to find out exactly what he had to offer. As soon as we entered the room, we started jumping on each other. We were like two horny high school kids that were trying to hurry up and get it in before their parents came home. He gently laid me down on the luxurious king size mattress and removed my shoes. He started massaging my feet and gazed deep into my eyes. He removed my pants and started kissing all around my legs and thighs. My breathing sped up as he got closer to my sweet spot and started to lightly blow on it. He must have been giving me a little teaser because he moved from that spot and came back up to my neck.

He ran his tongue from my neck, down to my collar bone and chest. I almost went crazy when he started nibbling on my ear. He was taking his time with me and being so passionate and seductive. He took a second to stand back and admire my body which was clad in red lace boy shorts and a matching bra.

"Are you sure that you're ready to do this? You know I ain't in no rush," he said.

I couldn't believe it, Milan had this man all to herself and she hadn't given up the cookies yet? *"Looks like I'm gonna leave my imprint on ya man before you do, bitch,"* I thought.

"I've never been more sure about anything in my life," I responded.

Those were the last words I spoke before he was tonguing me down once again. The man kissed me all over my body, not missing a single spot. He was making love to my body with his mouth and I was loving every minute of it. I couldn't take any more of the teasing, so I got up and motioned for him to lie down. I got on top of him and slid down his pole. As soon as I got the whole thing in my juices squirted all over him. He had a curve in his thick, long dick so as soon as it went in he hit my g–spot. I started off slow winding on the dick.

I worked his pole like a stripper at a club and he was enjoying that shit. He grabbed my waist and started to move me up and down faster, so I took over and started to bounce up and down like I was riding a mechanical bull. He pushed his dick further into me like he was trying to touch my soul. It damn near brought me to tears. He was fucking me so good. After about five more minutes we climaxed simultaneously. I suddenly realized that we hadn't even thought about protection. He had just shot a load of semen up in me. I didn't even care at the moment, though because I was so caught up in the aftermath of our ecstasy.

He slid his boxers back on, grabbed a blunt that had already been rolled and went out to the balcony. I wrapped the sheet around me and followed him. The breeze felt wonderful and the view we had from the 16th floor was breath taking. As he lit the blunt and inhaled, I wrapped my arms snuggly around his waist from behind and pressed my cheek against his chiseled back. I inhaled the captivating scent of this man whose name I didn't even know. Milan was dumb as hell because even I knew that what you wouldn't do the next bitch would. While she was trying to hold out, I bet her man was out there fucking somebody else.

"I would allow you to hit my shit, but the last time I did, you started tweaking out. I thought I was going to have to take your ass to the hospital. You were tripping so hard." He busted out laughing at the memory that I knew absolutely nothing about. I just flicked him off and gave him a cute smile. I didn't know the story, but it sounded like something that would be embarrassing to Milan if it was ever brought up again. So I just played it off.

"That's okay, I'm already high off you," I said, seductively.

He put the musty smelling weed out and pulled me into the warmest embrace I'd ever experienced. I had never been so comfortable in somebody's arms. He started kissing the back of my neck. Suddenly, he slid up inside of me from behind. He bent me over the rail of that balcony and fucked me like there was no tomorrow. I was pretty sure all the people in the rooms below us could hear my moaning and screaming, but I didn't give a damn. He was taking me higher than I had ever been in my life. I had only had two sex partners in my life, and neither of them had this kind of experience. It was like he was made to please me and only me. Milan would be lucky if she ever got her man back after tonight. After we finished our round on the balcony we went back into the room and made sweet tender love for the rest of the night. I knew that he was going to become my new addiction because he hadn't even left my side yet and I was already craving for more of him.

CHAPTER 11

Milan

I opened my eyes and squinted to adjust to the bright lights that were on in the room. I tried to get up from the hard chair I was sitting in only to find that my ankles were handcuffed to the legs of the chair and my arms cuffed behind my back. The last thing I remembered was running into London at Paradise. I looked around to see where the hell I was. It looked like I was in some type of cabin. There was a fireplace and hard wood floors in the living room that I was sitting in.

"What the fuck? Where am I? SOMEBODY HELP ME PLEASE!! HELP! HELPPPP!!!" I was screaming to the top of my lungs and desperately trying to get out of the chair, which I knew would be impossible.

It finally came back to me that Chief kidnapped me and I pulled out my gun on him. Next thing I knew his partner pulled out on me and knocked me out with a piece of cold steel.

Chief walked in the room with a smirk on his face. His presence alone caused the hairs on the back of my neck stand up. I wished I would have shot him when I had the chance because I had no idea what he was about to do to me. The only thing that stopped me from pulling that trigger was the fact that I knew I would die too, and I wasn't ready to die.

"SOMEBODY HELP ME!!!!" I cried.

I wasn't sure what was funny, but Chief let out one of those lunatic laughs, and it scared the hell out of me. "You can yell and scream all you want, but ain't nobody gonna hear you. It's just me and you out here all alone. Isn't this what you wanted Milan? You said you wanted to get away with me. You got what you wanted so what's the problem?"

The look in his eyes gave me chills. Something about his eyes was different, and it scared me. They reminded me of the nightmare that I had about him chasing me.

This crazy motherfucker has lost his damn mind.

I sat in silence because I didn't know what to do. I was defenseless and I knew that one wrong move could cost me my life. He was pacing back and forth in front of me and I never took my eyes off of him. The only thing you could hear was his footsteps and my unsteady, heavy breathing. While I was watching him I noticed how small he had gotten. He was still had his muscular build, but he looked like he lost at least twenty pounds. One side of his face was perfect, with his smooth, milky complexion. If you looked at him from that angle you would think that he was one of the sexiest men alive. The other side, however, looked horrific. It was a sight that would cause a child to run away and cry for their mommy. The cut had turned into a nasty looking keloid and it covered the entire right side of his face.

Chief stopped pacing and started to approach me. I was sweating bullets and damn near about to lose my breath in fear of what he was about to do. The closer he got to me, the more I got the urge to piss on myself.

"Why are you doing this to me Chief? What did I do to deserve this?" I whimpered.

"Nah don't cry now. You were just a gangsta bitch when you called yourself trying to kill me. I'm going to enjoy blowing your boyfriend's brains out in front of you. Don't worry though; you'll get to die with him."

"Elijah doesn't have anything to do with this leave him out of it!" The thought of him even touching a hair on Elijah's head had me ready to break out of those handcuffs and kill him with my bare hands.

"Trying to defend your boyfriend ain't gonna do shit but make you die faster, then he's still going to die. When he dies I'll be the plug around this bitch. It's time for me to move up in the game and I'm taking out anyone that gets in the way of that!"

"It's enough money in this world for everybody to eat; you don't have to kill nobody to get it. That man has been loyal to you, not to mention the deals you were getting on that white girl. Is this really how you're going to pay him back?"

I was hoping that I could talk some sense into Chief so I could make it out of there alive. It damn sure didn't seem like I was achieving that goal. If anything I was pissing him off even more.

"Ain't no loyalty in these streets. You should know that by now. Maybe you don't know because you're the snake that can't be trusted. Ain't that right Milan? "

I'm not anything like you Chief. I didn't even know that you could be this...this deranged maniac I'm looking at right now. I don't even recognize you and in all the time I have spent around you I have never seen this side of you."

"That just proves what I said to be true, ain't no loyalty in these streets. Nobody can be trusted. I'm not the person you thought I was, but that's just how it goes. Now enough with the small talk, let's play," the cynical laugh he let out and the psychotic look in his eyes told me that shit was about to get ugly.

I know I don't come to you as often as I should God but please, get me out of here.

I closed my eyes for a split second to say my silent prayers and as fast as I opened my eyes, Chief was standing right over me. My breathing became erratic and tears flowed down my face. I wanted to sniff the snot that was dripping down my nose, but I was too afraid to make a sudden move or sound. A grin spread across Chief's face like he was getting pleasure out of the fact that he was scaring me half to death.

Chief ran his fingers down my cheek and his touch made me cringe. He rubbed his hands through my scalp and then violently snatched my head back and made me look him in his face.

"I liked you Milan, I did. Then you started fucking up. For one, you didn't play your role like you should have. You know that you ain't my bitch, yet after we get caught you keep

164

running your mouth and telling it all. You wasted no time being a slut and hopping on the next nigga dick. That just so happened to be my connect, how ironic is that? You were a foul bitch for that one. The icing on the cake was when you tried to act like you were about to blow my head off. Now that was the wrong move, because I'm gonna make you pay for that. I like to eliminate my problems before they turn into bigger problems." Chief winked his eye at me and sent chills down my spine.

I was praying that somebody, anybody would save me. I knew that Elijah would figure that something was wrong when he kept getting my voicemail and saw that I hadn't been home.

As if he were reading my thoughts Chief said, "Ain't nobody gonna save you. It's just me and you."

"Please Chief, don't do this!"

He walked over to the fireplace and set it ablaze. He then grabbed a butcher knife from the mantle of the fireplace. My heart beat quickened when I saw the size of that blade. He was walking over to me slowly, purposely taking his precious time to torture me. He was getting a kick out of watching me squirm.

"Wait a minute Chief, I have something to tell you before you kill me!"

"I'm pretty sure whatever it is can wait until we meet again in hell," he put the tip of the knife on my neck and poked me lightly.

"NO Chief!!!! I'm pregnant and the baby is yours!"

"Bitch don't tell no lies like that. You know damn well that if you are pregnant that baby ain't mine!"

"What the fuck you mean it ain't yours Chief? You're the only person I been fucking for the past two years of course the baby is yours," I cried.

I was jumping out on a limb with that one, but I was willing to try anything at that point. I saw how he protected my mother because she was carrying his child and I figured he would do the same for me since I led him to believe I was carrying his seed.

I saw his face soften up a bit, but not enough to calm me down. He still had that look in his eyes so I didn't know what to think. Suddenly his phone rang and took his attention of me. He turned his back on me to tend to his phone call. I was too busy asking God to spare my life to pay attention to what he was saying. I had never prayed so much in my life. I didn't even know I knew how to pray, but desperate times called for desperate measures. I just hoped that it wasn't too late for me.

God must have been on my side for the moment because Chief hung up the phone and stormed out of the cabin. When I heard the front door slam, a car rev up, and tires screeching away, I finally let out a deep breath.

Now how the fuck am I going to get out of here?

CHAPTER 12

Silina

After having a dead bird sent to my job and my home broken into and trashed, I became way more cautious about how I moved. I filed a police report that very same day, but of course there wasn't much they could do because we didn't have a person of interest. I couldn't tell them that I suspected that my husband was trying to kill me to get revenge for being shot by my daughter. I took matters into my own hands when I decided to get surveillance cameras installed.

I was so on edge that the ringing of the doorbell made me jump. I figured that it was the technician coming to hook up my cameras. I went to the door and swung it open without ever looking out of the peephole.

I couldn't hide the shock on my face when I opened the door and saw who was actually standing behind it.

"What's the matter Silina, you look like you just saw a ghost."

I tried to slam the door shut, but before it could close all the way, he used his shoulder to force his way in.

"Why are you here? What do you want with me?"

"I came back to get what's rightfully mine. You didn't think that I wasn't going to come back for you, did you?"

"Please just leave. You aren't welcome here. You're no longer a part of my life, and I want to keep it that way!"

"Only if things were that simple," he said as he grabbed me harshly by my arm and pulled me to him.

I could smell the liquor on his breath when he got close enough to my face. He tried to force himself on me and I tried my hardest to fight him off. It wasn't too much that I could do being that I was now almost 8 months pregnant. The more I tried to get out of his grasp, the rougher he became. He hit me in my head with a blunt object, and it was lights out for me.

Tiana

My professor stopped me while I was walking out of class. "Tiana, can I speak to you for a moment?" I didn't really have a moment and I wasn't in the mood to bothered, but I decided not to be a bitch.

I looked at her and waited for her to talk because I didn't know what this was about.

"There was a note on the door when I got to class this morning, but it was addressed to you, so I didn't open it. I just wanted to give it to you," she stated, as she rummaged through a stack of papers on her desk.

A note addressed to me? I had no idea what the fuck that was all about so I snatched the envelope open right away when she handed it to me.

Your mama is a dead woman walking. Her time is almost up....

After reading that note all the blood drained from my face. My professor must have seen the look of horror in my eyes because she looked at me and asked me if I was going to be alright. I flew past her without saying a word and started running to get to my car. In the process of me making a mad dash to the parking lot, I took out my phone and dialed my mom's number. She didn't pick up, so I tried to call London. I couldn't get in touch with her either. I started to panic and my hands were trembling as I tried to get the key in the door lock. A piece of paper on my windshield caught my eye and I grabbed it before I got in. Before I started the car, I took a look at the paper.

Tick tock. Tick tock. Those were the only words that were on the piece of paper. I hauled ass out of the parking lot, so I could get home and make sure my mom was okay. I continually tried to get in contact with her but it was no use. I sensed that something was wrong because my mama always answered the phone, especially with everything that was going on. I hated the fact that it took me almost twenty minutes to get home from my school. I felt like I couldn't get to her fast enough, so I kept trying to call London to see if she was closer. She still wasn't answering either.

"Fuck! Why is this bitch not answering her phone? Calm down Tiana." I told myself.

Whoever was doing this was trying to torture all of us. All I could think about was Chief. The day that I shot him kept playing over and over in my head. I felt in my heart that he was the one behind all this.

"Obviously I didn't kill you last time, but this time you won't be able to get up, bitch ass nigga!" I screamed in frustration.

When I finally pulled up in front of my house, something seemed terribly wrong. The house was completely dark, but my mom's car was parked in the driveway. I got my glock from under my seat and cocked that bitch back, preparing to blow a nigga's brains out. I ran up to the door and entered the house quietly, so that I would have the element of surprise on my side. My mother wasn't anywhere in sight. I cut on all the lights downstairs and searched for her, but she wasn't there. Then I heard soft whimpers coming from upstairs. The closer I got to her room, the louder it became. I broke my neck trying to get to her, to see what was going on.

"Oh my goodness! Ma! What the fuck happened to you who did this?" I panicked.

My mom was sitting in a chair in her room with her hands tied behind her back and her feet tied together. She had a piece of tape covering her mouth. I noticed that she had a small cut on her head that was bleeding. I snatched the tape off of her mouth, and when she looked at me her eyes got wide with fear. Tears started streaming down her cheeks. Based on her reaction, I knew that someone was behind me. She started trembling like a baby duck that had been in the cold water for too long.

"If it isn't one of my favorite girls," I heard the voice behind me say.

I still hadn't turned around yet, I just stood there frozen in fear. I didn't know what to expect, so I didn't want to react too fast and make the wrong move. I had to be smart if I wanted my mom and me to make it out alive. Chills shot down my spine as I felt hot air breathing down my neck.

"No need to be afraid, you know you'll always be daddy's little girl."

I didn't even need to turn around to know exactly who was behind me. After all this time, the past had finally caught up with us. I guess it's true when they say you can't run forever. Somehow and some way, your demons would always find a way to catch up with you.

London

Waking up with my body nestled under Elijah's was an amazing feeling. I felt more comfortable than I ever had with a man before, too comfortable for my liking. Surprisingly Milan never came home, and I was hoping that she did so she could catch us in the act.

Bitch probably out being the hoe that she is.

The vibrating phone on the nightstand caught my attention and I realized that it was mine. I picked it up to find that I had 12 missed calls from Tiana. I also had a text message that had just come in from her.

Where are you? Answer the fucking phone mama needs us. Meet me at the house ASAP!!!!

I immediately hopped out of the bed and started searching for my clothes. Just when I was putting on my shoes and about to head out the door Elijah woke up.

"Where you headed to in such a rush?" he asked groggily.

175

"I have some business I need to handle but I'll be back soon."

I rushed out of the room and damn near sprinted out the front door before he could ask me anymore questions. I didn't have time for small talk, my family was in trouble. I hopped in my car and peeled out of the parking garage while trying to call Tiana back. This time she was the one not answering her phone. That made me worry even more and I put the pedal to the metal. I got home in record time, turning a 30 minute drive into a 15 minute one.

When I pulled up to the house I noticed that Tiana's car was parked in the driveway with the door slightly open. I decided to park around the corner so if something was going on I would have the element of surprise. I grabbed my pistol from under my seat and jogged back to our house. When I went to open the door I noticed that it wasn't all the way closed either. My nerves started to get the best of me when I realized that I didn't know what the hell I was walking into. I had to suck it up though because my mama needed me and I wasn't about to let anyone take her away from me.

As soon as I got in the house I heard soft whimpers. I tip toed through the foyer, careful not to alert any intruders that may have been in my home. I pointed my gun in front of me and prayed that I wouldn't have to use it, but something told me that I might as well get prepared for the worst. I knew damn well I wasn't a killer, but if I wouldn't hesitate to put a bullet in somebody for my mama. I was in complete shock at what I saw when I peeked around the corner into the kitchen.

My mama was tied up to a chair and her mouth was covered with tape. I could see that Tiana had her gun aimed at someone, but from the angle I was standing I couldn't see who the person was.

"If you shoot me, your mama is going with me. So think about that before your trigger finger starts itching," I heard a familiar voice say.

Stop being a bitch and go find out what the fuck is going on London!

As scared as I was, I proceeded to enter the kitchen. As soon as I stepped in, I was standing face to face with someone I thought I would never see again, my dad!

"Hey London, why don't you come give your daddy a big hug!"

"What the fuck are you doing here? Ain't you supposed to be rotting in prison?"

"Yeah well, let's just say some things worked out in my favor, now I'm here to tend to some unfinished business."

"Well you can carry your ass back to where you came from because you ain't wanted around here!"

"Y'all made that perfectly clear when y'all left me for dead in prison. If it wasn't for this pretty little lady right here I would have never served a day. She didn't even have the decency to answer a phone call, send a letter, or even visit. She snatched my kids out of my life," he said as he brought his gun up to the back of my mom's head.

She was so scared that she had urinated all over herself and was crying so hard that if it wasn't for the tape, she would have been eating snot. I heard the sound of Tiana cocking her gun back.

"Don't do it Tiana, just chill out for a second," I tried to reason with her. As much as I wanted her to shoot him, I knew that if she wasn't precise then that was our mother's ass.

I was shaking like a leaf the whole time. I had never seen so many guns in my life up until a few months ago. I wouldn't hesitate to fuck a bitch up, but I wasn't about that gun life. If it came down to my life or someone I loved, however, I would definitely pull that trigger.

"You better listen to your big sister!" he said.

"She didn't snatch us out of your life; we made that decision on our own. None of us like your ass and we would have been pleased to see you in a casket. You're a sorry excuse for a man, putting your hands on a woman every day. I bet they had fun with you in prison huh lover boy?" Tiana smirked. I loved the fact that she always said the first thing that came to her mind, but under those circumstances I prayed that she would shut the fuck up and not make things worse.

Tiana never took her gun off of him, and I got this déjà vu feeling. I was giving my baby sis the side eye because she was getting a little too comfortable with that gun. Then it dawned on me…Chief was never behind any of this. It was our dad the whole time!

Our dad took the gun from our mother's head and aimed it at Tiana. I just knew some wild Wild West shit was about to go down. Tiana was gripping the gun so hard that I could see the veins in her hand popping out. Our mother was sitting in the chair defenseless, watching everything transpire. I knew that she was begging and pleading with our father, but only muffled sounds and heart wrenching cries could be heard. I didn't know what the hell to do, so I aimed my gun at him too.

"Put the gun down," I said through a clenched jaw.

He looked at me like I had lost my mind when in all reality he was the crazy one.

"I'll die for my mama but trust and believe I'm taking you out with me," I warned him.

He looked back and forth between me and Tiana and I could tell that he didn't know what his next move was going to be. He knew that there was no way out of that. His eyes were fixated on Tiana and me as he put his arm around our mother's neck and put the gun to her head once again. She was shaking her head no and trying her hardest to scream through the tape. She even struggled to try to get her hands loose, but her efforts were futile.

"If I go, she's coming with me. Y'all mother is a sorry excuse for a woman. If it wasn't for her I would have never done any time upstate. I know this dirty lil' bitch snitched on me. She had it all planned out and set up, I know she was working with the FEDS. You have no idea what I went through when I was locked up, but she's about to find out when she rots in hell!" he snapped, directing his last statement towards my mother.

"I have a pretty good idea of what you went through and you deserved every bit of it. I hope you were violently sodomized every single night. You're nothing but a bitch ass nigga. You are the worst type of scum that I have ever seen in my life. You knocked my mama upside her head for countless years but you couldn't stand up to them niggas in jail huh? Only pussy's beat up on women, because they're too scared to fight a man. You disgust me. You ain't a man, *you're* the sorry excuse," Tiana said, gun still drawn.

POW! POW! Two shots rang out, followed by three more. I wasn't sure at the moment but I swore the second set of shots came from behind me. The first two shots hit Tiana and she fell to the ground like a sack of potatoes. Next thing I knew our father took two to the head and one to the chest. I believed he was dead before he even hit the ground. My mother and I were screaming to the top of our lungs, even though her screams were stifled. Out of the corner of my eye I saw a figure moving past me, so I automatically raised my gun and got ready to fire.

"Don't shoot, it's me. I'm here to help y'all. I shot him for you!" he said, putting his hands up in a "don't shoot" manner.

I almost passed out when I realized that it was Chief. After all the time that went by without us knowing what happened to him, he was standing right there in the flesh. He wasted no time tending to my mother. I ran straight over to Tiana who was bleeding profusely from her stomach.

"Oh my God somebody get help. Stay with me baby sis stay with me!"

I wanted to pick her up and cradle her in my lap but I was afraid that if I moved her I would fuck her up even more. I heard Chief on the phone with the 911 dispatcher so I kept talking to Tiana.

"It hurts," she whispered. Tears were flowing down her face and she started choking on her blood.

"No, baby girl, don't do this. You gotta stay with me. Me and mama need you to help us with your baby brother. You have to be here for him Tiana; you have to be here for us. Please fight Tiana, help is on the way. Don't leave me baby girl, don't leave me!!" My tears splashed off her freckles and mixed with hers. I was squeezing her hand tightly, hoping that my words would give her enough reason to fight. I was wailing so hard that my stomach started to hurt and I couldn't breathe. I couldn't lose my baby sister. She was all I had.

I didn't know if seconds or minutes went by, but Chief had freed my mother from the rope she was tied up with and the tape. The cry of a mother watching her child suffer in pain was nothing like I had ever heard before. It hurt me to my soul to hear those piercing screams. Chief wrapped his arms around her to console her, and she melted into his chest and released every bit of pain that was within her. The agony we were experiencing at that moment was something I will never forget.

Before the paramedics or police showed up, Chief unenthusiastically released his hold on my mom. While I was going to comfort my mom Chief grabbed Tiana's gun, ran out of the back door, and hauled ass. Seconds later we heard sirens approaching. The paramedics burst through the front door and efficiently placed Tiana on a gurney.

"She has a pulse!"

By this time they were running back out of the door with Tiana and the stretcher, with my mom and I hot on their trail.

"Excuse me ladies, you're going to have to let us do our job," one of the male paramedics stopped us.

"I'm coming with her; I'm not leaving my daughter's side!"

"If you're her parent then you are allowed to ride in front of the ambulance ma'am," he paused and looked at me. "But you're going to have to meet us at the hospital."

My mom got in the ambulance and they sped off, the sirens soon fading into the background. I didn't waste any time going back towards the house so I could get my car keys and get to the hospital. Before I knew it police officers, detectives, and forensics were flooding our home. I knew for a fact that our daddy was dead because when I walked in the kitchen, his body was still on the floor, eyes wide open. The forensics team was examining the crime scene so nobody was paying me any mind. I got my car keys off the floor and turned right back around to go to the hospital. As soon as I was on my way out the door...

. "I'm Detective Donna Hughes with Chesapeake P.D. I need to ask you a few questions about what went on here this morning. Do you have a moment?" An older black lady asked me. The only thing that gave away her age was the gray streaks in her jet black hair and the crow's feet around her eyes.

"I really don't have time right now I have to get to the hospital with my sister and my mom. My sister was shot, I have to go!"

"Unfortunately you don't have a choice young lady. You're not going anywhere until you answer our questions," a tall white man with blond hair and blue eyes said.

I know I just told these motherfuckers my sister got shot. Did this bitch just have the nerve to get irate with me after I told him that? Oh hell nah.

"Excuse me? Did you just tell me I couldn't leave? My sister is in an ambulance bleeding to death!"

"Ma'am, we just need to know what happened here this morning. The faster you answer our questions, the quicker you'll be on your way," the lady said in a much nicer tone than her douche bag partner.

"The man that's lying dead in the kitchen was sending my mama death threats. She reported both incidents to the police but of course y'all don't take anything serious until it's too late. Anyway, I came home this morning to find that he had my pregnant mother tied up to a chair and both she and my baby sister were being held at gun point. He saw me come in the

187

kitchen and he shot my sister. I didn't get to see who shot him because I immediately dropped to my knees and started crawling towards my sister, but I heard footsteps and saw someone running past out of the corner of my eye. They came and went so fast, but somebody definitely ran in here through the front, shot him, and left out of the back door." I didn't tell on Chief because if it wasn't for him we would have probably all been dead. "Can I go now?"

"You mean to tell me somebody just ran through your front door, shot this man, and left? And you didn't know this person? It was just a right place, right time type of thing?" the man asked me.

"That's exactly what I'm telling you."

He looked at me suspiciously and I looked him right back in his eyes because I knew I hadn't done anything wrong.

"What was this man's name?" the lady asked.

"Shawn Gellar, he was my father."

"Shawn Gellar? You mean the one that left the halfway house on 20th Street and had a warrant out for his arrest because he never returned?"

"I didn't know about any half way houses or none of that. I was under the impression that he was released from prison on good behavior. You can see for yourself if he fits the description, but I only know one Shawn Gellar and that's him. I don't know anything else, so can I go now?"

"Go ahead, you're family needs you. Take this and give me a call if you happen to remember anything else," she handed me her card with her cell and office number on it.

The male detective was still looking at me funny. I didn't know what his problem was, but I had a feeling that I wouldn't be seeing the last of him. I wasn't worried though, because there was no way he could tie me to that murder. I didn't do it.

As soon as I got around the corner to my 2014 Honda Accord I threw the card the detective gave me on the ground. I damn sure wouldn't be using it. I burned rubber trying to get to the hospital as fast as I could.

"God please let my sister make it through this. She doesn't deserve to die," I prayed out loud. My emotions tried to get the best of me once again but I had to be strong for my mother. She was the one who really needed somebody to lean on.

Right before I pulled up to Chesapeake General Hospital I heard sirens approaching from behind. I took me foot of the accelerator to slow down because I was doing 65mph in a 45mph zone. I didn't even realize that I was the one being pursued until I heard a voice speak into the bullhorn.

"PULL OVER AND STEP OUT OF THE VEHICLE!"

"What the fuck?"

I reluctantly pulled over to the side of the road and stepped out of the car with my hands up. I didn't want to become a victim of police brutality so I made sure I showed them that I did not have any weapons on me. As soon as I got out, I saw male detective that was just at our house approaching me.

I knew this motherfucker was going to be a pain in my ass!

"What can I help you with now sir?" I questioned.

"You can start by explaining this gun that we found at the scene of the crime. This wouldn't happen to be yours, would it?"

I was at a loss for words. I couldn't believe that I was stupid enough to leave the damn gun. Even though it was legally registered to me, I didn't have time for all the technicalities that would come with proving that. The only thing I had time for was being by my baby sister's side.

"No, it ain't mine and I don't know who it belongs to," I lied, hoping that he would just leave me alone.

"Well since you don't know who it belongs to, you'll be coming with us. We have a dead man and a young lady in critical condition and the only gun that was found at the scene was this one. Since you were the only one at the scene when we arrived, you are considered a prime suspect. We are taking you downtown to have you finger printed and if your prints match those on the gun, you're going down!"

He didn't even let me respond before he slapped cuffs on my wrist, opened the door to the police car and shoved me in the backseat. As we rode down to the precinct, the only thing I could think about was Tiana's condition. I didn't know if she was dead or alive, and that was burning me up inside. I would never forgive myself if my sister left this earth and I wasn't by her side. If that was the case, there would definitely be hell to pay and that relentless ass detective would be the one to have to pay the cost.

to be continued...

About the Author:

Jasmine M. Williams, born and raised in Virginia Beach, VA, is a mother of two with a passion for writing. Her knack for writing started in middle school when she and a classmate used to be in competition of who could write the best short stories. Reading the novel "The Coldest Winter Ever" by Sista Souljah inspired her to want to write a story of her own. All the obstacles that life threw her way and becoming a mother at an early age didn't deter her dreams; it made her fight harder to make them a reality. She aspires to become a full time author and to see one or more of her books hit the silver screen. While she is writing and being a full time mother, she is also working on getting her Bachelor's degree in Business Management.

Follow the author:

Instagram: @classy_jazzy_
Twitter: @1classy_JAZZY
Facebook: facebook.com/1classyjazzy

CPSIA information can be obtained at www.ICGtesting.com
Printed in the USA
LVOW10s1747071016

507864LV00014B/916/P

9 781512 181692